"You're not indispensable,"

Shad said. "Not to a company, not to a client. But to him—" he jerked a thumb in the direction of her son and the family room "—right now, you *are* indispensable." He leaned closer. Too close for either one of them to deal with objectively.

J.T. held her ground, her knees weak. "Just how many kids do *you* have?"

"None," Shad answered casually. "But I was one once."

J.T. didn't want to know anything about his childhood. Knowing would weaken her. He'd become more of a person, a friend, a—

Slowly, so slowly that it felt as if time had stood still, he lowered his mouth to hers. And then his lips touched hers so softly that she ached inside.

"What was that for?" J.T. asked in a whisper.

"Openers...."

Dear Reader,

The summer is over, it's back to school and time to look forward to the delights of autumn—the changing leaves, the harvest, the special holidays . . . and those frosty nights curled up by the fire with a Silhouette Romance novel.

Silhouette Romance books always reflect the laughter, the tears, the sheer joy of falling in love. And this month is no exception as our heroines find the heroes of their dreams—from the boy next door to the handsome, mysterious stranger.

September continues our WRITTEN IN THE STARS series. Each month in 1991, we're proud to present a book that focuses on the hero—and his astrological sign. September features the strong, enticingly reserved Virgo man in Helen R. Myers's *Through My Eyes*.

I hope you enjoy this month's selection of stories, and in the months to come, watch for Silhouette Romance novels by your all-time favorites including Diana Palmer, Brittany Young, Annette Broadrick and many others.

We love to hear from our readers, and we'd love to hear from *you!*

Happy Reading,

Valerie Susan Hayward
Senior Editor

MARIE FERRARELLA

Man Trouble

Silhouette *Romance*

Published by Silhouette Books New York

America's Publisher of Contemporary Romance

To Melissa Senate,
and to new beginnings and new friendships

SILHOUETTE BOOKS
300 E. 42nd St., New York, N.Y. 10017

MAN TROUBLE

Copyright © 1991 by Marie Rydzynski-Ferrarella

ISBN: 0-373-08815-9

First Silhouette Books printing September 1991

MARIE FERRARELLA

was born in Europe, raised in New York City and now lives in Southern California. She describes herself as the tired mother of two overenergetic children and the contented wife of one wonderful man. She is thrilled to be following her dream of writing full-time.

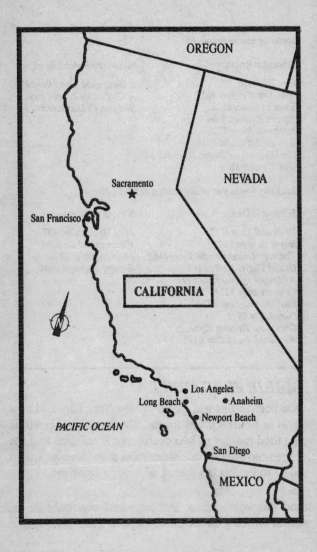

Chapter One

How had he let himself get talked into this?

Shad pressed down on the accelerator and maneuvered his car into an opening in the adjacent lane. He breathed a sigh of relief as the car behind him slowed down just a few feet from his bumper. Rush-hour traffic on the 405 was always guaranteed to get blood pumping and adrenaline flowing. Especially at five-thirty in the afternoon.

The question rattled through Shad's mind again as he contemplated the alternative to his present position: sitting back in his Jacuzzi, relaxing his aching, overworked muscles and sipping something tall and cool.

Anything tall and cool, he thought irritably as he pressed the button on his control panel and rolled down the windows on either side of him. His car's air-conditioning always seemed to malfunction on the hottest days. And it was ninety today, with no relief in sight for hours. The cooling trend the weatherman had promised was only so much wishful thinking on the bureau's part. Shad felt a trickle of perspiration work its way down his spine and he swore under his breath.

He was hot, tired and thirsty. And he wanted to go home.

But grumble though he did, Shad knew *exactly* how he had been talked into driving on the freeway at this hour in the exact opposite direction from his home. His sun-darkened, chiseled-out-of-granite profile framed with thick black hair that came by way of distant Cherokee blood spoke of a strong-willed, confident man. Maybe the drilled-in cleft chin and single dimple in his right cheek might have given people a moment's wavering as to his disposition. But ultimately everyone he came in contact with knew that Shadrach Michael McClellan had always been his own man, for as long as he could remember. He certainly wasn't a pushover.

Except where Dottie was concerned.

Diminutive, as petite and fair as he was brawny, tall and dark, she was the only one who could wrap him around her little finger. Oh, they had had their moments and their differences. But he had only one little sister. And this afternoon he had been so grateful to find out that she had emerged from the two-car pileup with only a broken leg that he would have promised to carry her piggyback down Wiltshire Boulevard if she had asked him to.

Fortunately for him she hadn't. But what she had asked him to do was just as arduous for him, considering the kind of a day it had been. Arduous and a little out of his league. Or a lot out of his league, he thought dryly, searching for another opening in traffic.

Why the hell did Dottie always get involved in these kinds of things?

He pushed a thatch of damp, wayward hair out of his eyes and scanned the lane on his right impatiently. He needed the right lane and soon. His exit was coming up. Or rather, the exit Dottie was to have taken if she and her now-defunct car were able.

She had an appointment to meet a Mrs. Mayne, who was a friend of a friend, or something like that. It seemed that Mrs. Mayne had her hands full with a contrary preteen son; and Dottie, big-hearted fledgling child psychologist that she was, had volunteered her services to see if something was *really* bothering the boy or if this was just the usual thing to be expected at his age. It wasn't even, he had learned, the first time she had done this sort of thing. Dottie was always rushing in where angels and sane people feared to tread. Thinking back, he vaguely remembered her saying something about giving more of herself, but he had thought she was talking about getting another pet, of which, in his estimation, she already had too many.

Pets. Damn. He remembered that he had also promised Dottie to stop by the apartment and feed that growing menagerie of hers. The Jacuzzi and his drink seemed further and further out of reach.

Shad saw his chance and took it, much to the annoyance of the black Porsche that was now queued up behind him closer than a moving vehicle had the right to be. He saw the driver glare at him in his rearview mirror and ignored the man. He was already late for Dottie's appointment, and the sooner he got that over with, and fed those animals of hers, the sooner he'd be in his Jacuzzi. He and his nerves deserved it.

First his roofer had called in sick, then he had learned about Dottie's accident. He'd been tied up in knots ever since he had gotten the call earlier this afternoon from Angelo at the hospital. His foster brother's agitation had done nothing to calm his nerves, until he arrived at the hospital himself. He *knew* his sister drove that Corvette of hers too fast. Leadfoot, that was what he had always called her affectionately. Well, no more. When she got well, he'd get her a scooter. The kind that got its power from a foot pushing along the sidewalk as the traveler held on to the handle-bars.

Shad had a mental image of Dottie, getting around by scooter and heaping curses on his soul. He grinned. It would serve her right. Scared him out of ten years, she had.

He sighed and told himself that it was going to be all right. The worst was over. But it was still hard for him to relax. His six-foot frame felt tense from the roots of his hair to the tips of his expensive hand-tooled leather boots.

The doctors had told him that Dottie was going to be fine, and that was all that mattered. He'd call the hospital later on tonight and check in on her after he fed her animals.

He glanced at the phone in his car. Why Dottie hadn't let him use the telephone to inform Mrs. Mayne and her son of the sudden change in plans was beyond him. But she had insisted. That was Dottie, considerate of others to the end—even if it meant that he was the one who had to do the work.

He wondered if Dottie appreciated him.

Julienne Trent Mayne discreetly raised the cuff of her silk blouse and glanced at her wristwatch, trying not to be obvious.

Where *was* the woman?

She looked at her son sitting on the sofa that bordered the large bay window. He held a magazine in his hands and was paging through it slowly. J.T. wasn't fooled. The boy was trying valiantly not to appear to be sneaking covert peeks out of the window. But he was.

J.T. felt slightly encouraged. And impatient. She wished the woman would get here. When they had spoken on the telephone yesterday, Dottie McClellan had suggested taking Francis to the ball game to break the ice. When J.T. mentioned it to her son, the boy had displayed a spark of his old enthusiasm. J.T. didn't want that to fade again. Above all else, J.T. didn't want Francis disappointed.

"She probably just got stuck in traffic." J.T. smiled soothingly. She sat down on the sofa next to Francis, trying to ignore the tension she felt. She was tense not because some stranger was late, but because she was around her own son.

When had it happened? She had wondered that so often in the past few months that she had lost count of the number of times the question had haunted her. When had this awkwardness slipped in between them, driving a wedge that grew wider with each passing day? They'd been so happy once, so attuned to each other. Now if she said "day," Francis would snap "night." She thought this was just a phase the boy was going through, but she wanted to be sure. J.T. wondered if she would survive her son's teen years. It didn't look very hopeful.

Her son shot her an annoyed look that came from beneath wispy blond bangs. His father's hair, J.T. thought. The memory brought no fond nudgings of nostalgia. Just a deadness. J.T. pushed it aside as carefully as she pushed aside scrap paper on her desk.

Francis let the magazine drop to the coffee table. "I don't care if she doesn't ever get here. It was a dumb idea, anyway." He hid his disappointment behind the blasé attitude of a twelve-year-old who was stuck in a time warp between child and man.

J.T. struggled not to be annoyed with Francis's tone of voice. Her patience was running on the thin side this afternoon. She had already put in a ten-hour day, arriving at her office at six in the morning to begin untangling the Grimes account. Grimes's former accountant had played fast and loose with the firm's money, which was why he was now getting his mail at the state prison and why, after some fancy promises, she had landed the account. She had brought the bulging file home with her, intending to work on it once Francis and the now very late Dottie McClellan were on their way to the ballpark. Jane Rollins had only glowing words to say about Dottie, telling her how wonderful she was about understanding teenagers, but J.T. intended to talk to the woman and judge for herself before she entrusted her with her son.

If she ever got here.

J.T. stifled an urge to pace. She wasn't good at waiting.

Maybe Francis was right. Maybe it was a dumb idea. But she was desperate enough to try anything, and when Jane had told her about Dottie, about the way the young woman could just make a teenager's best qualities bloom, J.T. had decided to call Dottie and explain her problem. Dottie had been more than happy to help.

Her main problem, J.T. thought, was just when her business was at a crisis point and needed her total attention, so did her son. The only difference was that the business was responding to the efforts she was putting out. Francis wasn't. J.T. had tried talking, she had tried not talking. Nothing seemed to work. Maybe an outsider would see something she didn't.

"For heaven's sake, send the boy to a boarding school," Adriana had instructed simply, as if her nephew was some sort of pet to be sent away if it displeased its owner.

For once J.T. had blocked out her older sister's words. She didn't want to send Francis away. Francis was the reason for everything, the reason she was working so hard, trying so hard. He was the reason she had pulled her life together after Pete left. There *had* to be a way to open up lines of communication again, to make her son realize that she cared about him. Until the time came when she could do that herself, J.T. was willing to allow a surrogate to fill that place for her. Anything not to lose Francis any more than she already had.

Frankie shifted moodily on the sofa. "I don't see why I have to talk to anyone just to make you happy. If she gets here, *you* can have her." Abruptly Frankie got off the sofa and started for the stairs.

J.T. rose. "Where are you going?"

"To get my ball and bat."

"Why?"

Francis frowned. "Because you can't play baseball without them."

J.T. struggled to control her temper. She knew Francis didn't like explaining his every move. "Don't get insolent with me."

"I'll get anything I want to," the boy retorted hotly. "Haven't you got a client to see or something?"

J.T. looked down at her watch. "As a matter of fact—" She looked up and saw the satisfied smirk on Francis's face as if he had known it all along. J.T. curled her fingers into her palms and dug in. "We're supposed to be waiting for Dottie McClellan. She's taking you to the ball game, remember?"

Frankie turned away. "You go."

"You're the one who likes baseball."

Frankie looked over his shoulder. "So you noticed something about me."

"What's that supposed to mean?"

"If you can't figure it out, never mind." The slender boy began to storm off to his room.

J.T. was right behind him, intent on having it out, when there was a knock on the front door. "Finally," she muttered. "Francis—"

"Frankie," her son corrected tersely.

"Whoever you are, come back here. Now." Sulking, Francis obeyed.

The housekeeper emerged from the kitchen to answer the door. "That's all right, Norma. I'll get it."

The heavyset woman nodded and willingly retreated back to the kitchen. The theme song from yet another rerun of *Happy Days* was heard wafting into the living room from that direction.

"Now I want you to behave," J.T. ordered sternly as she opened the door.

"I'll try, ma'am."

The deep, masculine voice startled her, and she swung around to look at the person standing in front of her. "I, um, didn't mean you."

Confusion and embarrassment surged through her. She stared at the man on her doorstep. She heard Francis's footsteps on the tile as the boy edged over for a closer look. J.T. kept her hand firmly on the doorknob as she composed herself. Clashes of will with Francis always drained her. "May I help you?"

Classy. That was the word that sprang instantly to mind, Shad thought. Very, very classy. The lady who opened the door was definitely something to look at. The face was slim, the cheekbones high, the eyes almond-shaped and a pale, almost translucent blue. Her deep chestnut hair was pulled back away from her face and was tightly secured. He wondered what it would look like, loose, free. Was it as thick and soft as it looked? Did it fall in waves, or was it straight? Almost unconsciously Shad made a mental note to find out. For a moment her generous mouth made him lose his train of thought. But only for a moment.

The lady, he told himself, most certainly merited closer scrutiny.

No one could ever accuse Shad of letting grass grow under his feet. He was used to making split-second decisions. He made one now.

He glanced at the address in his hand, then up at J.T. His smile was wide, guileless. "You're expecting a Dottie McClellan."

"Yes," J.T. began, then her eyes narrowed as she looked at him. "What about it?"

She was aware of the sudden interest Francis was displaying in the stranger as the boy jockeyed at her elbow for a better view. J.T. relented only a fraction as she eased the door open a little bit wider. A policeman lived across the street. If need be, she could scream with the best of them. Simon would be at her front door in a matter of seconds, glad to play the rescuer. He'd been trying to get to first base with her since he had moved in six months ago.

Shad gave Frankie a quick, cursory smile, but his attention was clearly riveted on J.T. "I've come to take her place."

"Excuse me?" J.T. kept her eyes on his face and a firm grip on the door.

Shad liked to think he was a good judge of people. He was also a *quick* judge of people. He liked what he saw. A lot. Dottie, never at a loss for words no matter what the circumstances, had convinced him, from her hospital bed, to deliver her apologies—and the baseball tickets—in person.

Because Dottie was always doing half a dozen things at once, she had accidentally gotten three tickets for tonight's game instead of two. For once, he mused, one of her mistakes was going to turn out all right. Suddenly his Jacuzzi wasn't nearly so appealing any more. Not as appealing as the woman in front of him. He had a sudden craving to see a ball game. Shad ran his hand over the back of his neck as he glanced up at the sky. "It's kind of hot, standing out here in the sun. Mind if I come in?"

"I'm not in the habit of inviting strange men into my house." She didn't budge, even though Francis tugged on her arm. Francis, it seemed, *liked* the man. He was entirely too trusting. What was she going to do with the boy?

Shad nodded. "Very good habit," he commended amiably.

J.T. felt her teeth getting on edge. "Thank you. Your approval means everything to me." She began to close the door. Somehow this man had found out that Dottie McClellan was coming to see Francis. She had no idea how he had gotten the information; moreover, she didn't *care* how he had gotten the information. She just wanted him off her doorstep.

Now.

She couldn't explain just why, but he made her nervous.

Shad put his hand on the door, and she had a feeling he could hold the door open no matter how much force she exerted to close it. She glanced over at Simon's house. The garage door was closed and there were no signs of life. It figured. The one time she wanted the man, he wasn't home.

"What is it you want?" J.T. wondered if Norma would hear her if she screamed. Probably not. The woman kept the sound high on that TV set of hers so that she could hear it over the noise of the appliances.

Maybe he should start over. Shad dug into the back pocket of his jeans and took out his wallet. "You were expecting Dottie McClellan, right?"

J.T. raised her chin. Suspicion highlighted the delicate features of her face. "Yes, we've already established that."

A man could freeze from that much ice if he wasn't careful, Shad thought. Lucky for him he was frost-proof. He flipped open his wallet and showed her his driver's license. "I'm her brother, Shad. Dottie's been in an accident."

J.T. looked at the picture on his license, read the name and then relaxed her hold on the front door. "Oh, I'm so sorry. Won't you come in?"

So, she had compassion beneath that suspicion. That was reassuring. He smiled at her engagingly and put out his hand. "Well, you know my name, Mrs. Mayne. It's only fair that I know yours." It was a small detail Dottie had overlooked, not that it had mattered at the time. It did now.

J.T. hesitated, then put her hand in his. "J.T." His hand felt strong, rough, like a laborer's hand, yet there was a gentleness in his grip. Questions stirred vaguely in her mind as she studied him.

Shad raised an eyebrow. "J.T.?"

"Yes."

"Do those initials stand for something?"

"Most initials do," she said smoothly, withdrawing her hand just as smoothly and letting it drop to her side. She saw his mouth open to ask the logical question and decided to change the subject. "Is it serious?" The word *accident* conjured up all sorts of terrible images in her mind.

"That remains to be seen." His eyes held hers, and she knew they were *not* talking about the same thing. As a matter of fact, she wasn't sure *what* he was talking about and had a strange feeling she didn't want to know.

"I was asking about the accident."

"Well, for the car it was terminal. For Dottie, fortunately, it was just a broken leg. But she's not going to be able to make it."

J.T. folded her hands in front of her, lacing her fingers together. She looked disheartened but resigned. "No, of course not."

Shad looked around the room. It was open, airy and welcoming, yet the woman was portraying herself as the exact opposite. Why? "She wanted me to come and tell you in person so that your son wouldn't feel he was being ignored or just fluffed off."

Her smile was strained, disappointed. "That was very nice of her, wasn't it, Francis?" She turned toward her son, who was staring at Shad unabashedly.

The name and the boy didn't seem to fit, Shad thought. The slight blond boy, who at first glance looked almost like a mirror image of his mother despite the different hair color, was wearing torn jeans and an Angels T-shirt. His mother was dressed as if she had just returned from a business meeting. A long, drawn-out, stuffy business meeting. He thanked the gods who had allowed him to make his living away from fluorescent lights and desks with no windows in sight.

"My name's Frankie," Frankie told him. The glance he spared his mother was impatient.

The look wasn't wasted on Shad. He nodded approvingly at the information and put out his hand to shake Frankie's. "Suits you."

His comment pleased Frankie as did his treatment. He shook hands with him. Suddenly shy, he stuck his hands into his back pockets as he shifted forward slightly. "We were supposed to go to a ball game."

Because he was twelve he pouted. Shad reached over and tugged at a strand of hair. "Well, the tickets didn't get hurt." He pulled them out of his pocket and held them aloft. Frankie's eyes lit up instantly. That cinched it for Shad.

Frankie needed nothing more. "I'll get my cap," he cried, and dashed off to his room.

J.T. hadn't seen such an unabashed display of enthusiasm on Francis's part in a long time. She felt a pang that someone other than she had brought it about. Then she turned to look at Shad. Enthusiasm or not, there was no way she could allow this man to take her son anywhere. "No, I'm sorry, Mr. McClellan—"

"Shad—"

Did she imagine it, or had he somehow managed to move closer to her without actually taking a step? J.T. could have sworn the air was growing a little warmer, as well. "Shad?"

His smile grew wider, warmer. "Like in the Bible— Shadrach, Meshach and Abednego."

Unconsciously she took a step back. "Yes, well, even if all three of you were here, I'm afraid I simply can't allow—"

He felt the refusal coming. To head it off Shad held up his hand. He hadn't learned to live off his wits for nothing. "I understand perfectly."

"You do?" She obviously hadn't given the man enough credit.

Frankie entered the room, his baseball cap on his head. He had managed to hear the tail end of the conversation. "Mother." He put his fisted hands on his hips and glared his disappointment.

Shad turned toward the boy and saw the scowl. Restrained thunder. He had a feeling this was what J.T. looked like when she became angry. "There's no harm in your mother coming with us, Frankie," he said soothingly. "She might learn something."

J.T. shook her head. "Oh, no, I didn't—"

Shad whipped around to look at J.T. "Want to impose. Sure, I understand," he assured her knowingly, "but since plans have changed this way, I can't see how you could help but go. As luck would have it, Dottie purchased three tickets."

For a moment J.T. felt as if she had been sucked into a whirlwind. It had to be those ten-hour days she was putting in. "As luck would have it," she echoed. Her voice rang in her ears, and she couldn't believe how dumb that sounded.

J.T. felt something heavy on her shoulders. His arm. How had he managed to slip an arm around her shoulders without her realizing it? It rested comfortably there as if they were old friends. "What time is the game?"

"Now." He laughed at the dazed look on her face.

His laugh was deep and rich and wound through her like the first cup of dark coffee in the morning, waking up all her senses.

He removed his arm from her shoulders for a moment to glance at his watch. "If we hurry, we have a very good chance of making the beginning of the game. Ready, Frankie?"

"You bet!"

J.T. couldn't find it in her heart to wipe the eager look from her son's face. Not twice. How bad could a baseball game be? "Just let me get my purse—" she began.

"Frankie, why don't you get your mother's purse?" Shad suggested.

He had but to ask and Francis was already moving. J.T. stared at the slight figure as it disappeared. To say she was stunned was a vast understatement.

"It's on the hall table," J.T. called out.

"I know."

For once there was no irritation in Francis's voice.

"Is this your first miracle, or do you perform them daily?" J.T. asked as she continued to look in the direction Francis had taken.

"Daily. Twice on Sundays. C'mon." He nodded toward the open doorway. "It's only fair that I drive."

She heard the grin in his voice and felt the arm around her shoulders again. Moving in a fog, J.T. let herself be ushered out to the Miracle Worker's car.

Chapter Two

Second thoughts came swiftly on the heels of the dazed, sudden impulse that had prompted J.T. to agree. Something told her that going off with this man was going to be a mistake. She hesitated, stopping abruptly at the car door. J.T. looked over her shoulder and saw Francis come flying out the front door.

"Here." The young boy quickly shoved J.T.'s purse into her hand and then, when J.T. stood motionless, tried to nudge his mother aside. Frankie gave her an accusing, perplexed look. "Mother, you're in my way."

"Famous last words," J.T. murmured. Mechanically she took a step back, allowing Francis to push the front seat down and climb into the back of the two-door car.

Her eyes locked with Shad's over the roof. His eyes were soft and gray, and she decided she couldn't really trust a man whose eyes made something inside of her feel like melted taffy. Melted taffy couldn't function, and above all else J.T. always needed to function.

Shad saw the misgivings in her eyes. He wasn't about to lose her now. "Something wrong?"

Yes. I'm running off to the ball game, or so you say, with a total stranger who could be who knows what.

J.T. shifted under Shad's gaze, feeling utterly vulnerable and annoyed with him for making her feel that way. She seized the first thing that came to mind.

"I'm really not dressed to go to a ball park." J.T. gestured at her suit. The simple statement was all she needed to cement her resolve. No more wavering. She was the adult. She would do what was right, even if it was unpopular with a certain blond-haired Angel fan.

J.T. leaned into the car, intent on taking Francis by force if necessary. They weren't going to a baseball game with an absolute stranger. It was totally inappropriate.

Shad saw the expression on her face harden. He couldn't just let things end like this. He knew he'd regret it. He had felt a strong and powerful attraction to this primly dressed woman the moment he'd seen her. He knew he'd have no peace unless he explored it. Instinct told him that. He had a healthy respect for instinct.

Quickly he was at J.T.'s side. He positioned himself to prevent her from physically dragging her son out of the back seat. Frankie watched with intense interest.

With a swift, thorough look that turned over all of J.T.'s nerve endings, Shad's eyes slid over her body. "I see your problem."

My problem is you, J.T. thought, annoyed and flustered at the same time. Her reaction reminded her too much of the way she had once been. The way she didn't want to be. Defenseless. Not in control. She suppressed an urge to physically push him out of her way. The impulse might have been curbed, but Shad could still see it in her eyes. "Well, then—"

"And it's too late to change clothes," he observed.

Finally she was getting through to him. "Yes, so we'll just take a raincheck—"

"Why don't you just take off your jacket and roll up your sleeves?" Before she could utter a sound, he began to help her off with her jacket.

Inside the car, Francis was making impatient noises, clearly wanting to be off. J.T. vaguely heard him. She was struggling with a very strong, very overwhelming feeling that she was being undressed by this tall stranger. Granted, he had moved the fabric only a fraction of an inch on her shoulders, yet the simple action felt incredibly intimate. J.T. felt something quivering inside of her.

Her verbal response was mechanical, completely devoid of self-assurance. "Roll up my sleeves?" J.T. glanced down at her arms, her expression almost bewildered. What was he doing to her? What was *she* doing to her? This was ridiculous. She had to snap out of it. "Do you have any idea how much this blouse cost?"

A slow, lazy smile transformed Shad's face into something out of every woman's fantasy. It was almost indescribably sexy. "Does it cost less if you don't roll up the sleeves?"

"No, of course not, but—" J.T. stopped, realizing how flimsy and ridiculous it all sounded.

Oh, what would it hurt? She was a grown woman. She could take care of herself. Almost as if she was challenging herself, J.T. acquiesced. With a huff that ruffled the tips of her bangs, she removed her linen jacket, unbuttoned the cuffs of her wine-colored silk blouse and neatly, precisely, folded up the right sleeve.

Watching her kindled the dormant fires of desire within Shad. At that moment both their fates were sealed. He knew that someday he'd watch her complete the ritual, watch her remove article after article of clothing slowly, deliberately, until there would be nothing left between them but the intense promise of passion. There was something very, very sensual about Ms. J. T. Mayne, although he'd be willing to bet money she wasn't aware of it.

"Mother." Frankie dragged out the name in obvious exasperation.

Shad took J.T.'s jacket from her and handed it to Frankie in the back seat. "C'mon," he urged, ushering J.T. into the car. "You can take care of the other sleeve on the way. We don't want to miss the game."

"Heaven forbid," J.T. muttered. Because her purse and son were already in the car, J.T. resigned herself to making the best of it and climbed into the front.

As Shad drove toward the freeway entrance, J.T. suddenly remembered the account she had brought home with her. The six-inch file that was lying on her desk in the den. The one she wasn't going to get to work on. And the client who went with the account. The one whose phone wasn't going to ring tonight.

Common sense reared its head and nagged at her. She should tell him to turn the car around and take them home. It was really the only logical thing to do. Francis could just wait until Dottie McClellan mended to go to a baseball game.

J.T. turned her head to deliver her edict, but the words evaporated on her lips.

Shad had a profile that could melt butter at forty paces, J.T. had to admit, provided the butter was of the female gender. J.T.'s eyes slid slowly over the man at her left, taking in his bone structure, his olive complexion, his chin. It was a strong chin that looked as if Shad McClellan took no nonsense from anyone.

Okay, fine, she thought, mechanically folding her other sleeve to match the one on her right arm. So people didn't walk all over him. She could appreciate that. But who *was* he? Besides Dottie McClellan's brother and a very smooth talker. She hadn't a clue and that just wasn't her way. J.T. never jumped into anything without thoroughly researching it from every angle. A disastrous marriage, entered into blindly with unfounded dreams, had taught her that.

So what was she doing, sitting in the front seat of a car being driven by a man she hadn't, half an hour ago, known from Adam? So he was cute. All right, more than cute. Stunning in a bone-melting way, but that wasn't a reason to trust him. There was no unwritten rule anywhere that said ax murderers were all ugly, and although something told her that he wasn't one of those, there was something *dangerous* about him. Something *personally* dangerous about him, although she couldn't quite put her finger on what.

"Who are you, Mr. McClellan?"

He had felt her eyes on him, but thought it best to wait and let her initiate the conversation. He wondered how long it would take her to get around to asking questions. She didn't look like the complacent type who could just be led around. The momentary distraction of giving in to her son wouldn't last long with a lady who didn't have one hair out of place on the hottest day of the year and who folded her sleeves as if the fate of the free world depended on it.

Shad guided the car onto the freeway entrance, then inclined his head toward her. "In what sense?"

J.T. frowned. "I beg your pardon?" The smile she had labeled as sexy became more so. She realized she was twisting the strap on her purse and stopped.

"Well, at the moment I'm just a guy taking my sister's place and driving a guy and his very attractive mother to what will hopefully be a great ball game." He turned slightly and winked at Frankie.

Frankie grinned and winked back.

Surprised at Francis's totally-out-of-character reaction, J.T. turned and stared at her son's face, then raised her eyes toward Shad. "When you're not driving to the ball game—" J.T. began and got no farther.

Bored by the conversation, Frankie interrupted with a question of far more urgency. He leaned forward and clutched his mother's headrest on either side with both hands, his eyes on Shad. "Do you think the Angels have a chance tonight?"

Shad glanced at J.T., made a judgment call and addressed himself to Frankie's question. He had a suspicion that Frankie might have been put on hold once too often when his questions interfered with adult conversations. Since he was taking them out for the evening, he was going to accomplish what Dottie had set out to do, or at least make a good dent in the problem he was beginning to perceive existed here.

"The Angels *always* have a chance." The huge arch of the letter *A* loomed ahead on the right side of the freeway, announcing their approach to Anaheim Stadium. Shad began to edge the car over to the right, jockeying for the next available opening in order to make the exit. Traffic slowed as a line of cars queued up for the same off ramp.

Everyone, Shad thought, seemed to be going to the ball game. "No matter what anyone says, they've always been a great ball club and this year, with that new kid they drafted pitching, I'd say—"

Oh, no, he wasn't going to shake her that easily, J.T. thought. She put her hand on his arm to draw his attention and emphasize her point. "I'd like an answer, Mr. Mc-

Clellan." It was the voice she used when she dealt with clients.

Shad glanced in her direction. "I am giving an answer, J.T.," he replied calmly. "To Frankie."

J.T. was about to tell him that her question was more important, but one glance at Francis's face told her that that would have been a huge mistake.

Okay, she thought, you win for now. But we'll get back to it.

J.T. crossed her arms and stared straight ahead. She was stuck for the time being and she knew it. But at least he had actually brought them to the stadium, not to some dark, subterranean cave the way she had feared he might. She had worried needlessly.

Relieved, she faced up to the prospect of being bored out of her mind. She braced herself as Shad eased the car into a parking space that appeared to be about a mile away from the stadium entrance. It looked as if all of Southern California had shown up for the game. Or at least that portion of the population that owned a car.

To her surprise Shad came around and opened the door for her. Okay, so he had manners. J.T. refused to take his offered hand as she got out. She had a feeling he was just doing it to win her over, and she wasn't about to be won. She'd endure this as long as she had to, for Francis's sake, and that would be that.

As she watched, Shad pushed forward the front seat and helped her son. Francis bounced out of the car, asking about the game, the players, the stadium, everything at once. He included J.T. in his exuberance, but it was clear that most of the nonstop barrage was aimed at Shad. Looking sideways, J.T. saw that the man seemed to be enjoying the bombardment.

Maybe he was just what he claimed to be, she thought, listening to Shad answer Francis's questions. Maybe he was just a man who was taking his sister's place in order not to disappoint a young boy.

She glanced at Francis's beaming face Heaven knows she couldn't fault him for that. Only for almost literally kidnapping her and forcing her to endure several hours of projected utter boredom. J.T. sighed, wishing she'd had the presence of mind to bring her briefcase with her. Then she could at least utilize the time they spent here instead of wasting it, waiting for a bunch of grown men to swing at a ball with a stick and get paid incredible amounts of money whether they hit it or not.

Shad noted the resigned look on J.T.'s face as he took her and Frankie by the arm, and placing himself in between, expertly guided them toward the entrance. It took some maneuvering in this crowd.

"Don't much care for the game, do you?" he asked J.T.

Frankie peeked around Shad's arm to look at his mother. "She hates it."

"Maybe that's because she doesn't understand it," he suggested to Frankie. "I think we should take pity on your mom and educate her about the fine art of this game. What d'you say?"

Francis grinned in response. J.T. felt another sharp pinch of jealousy that a total stranger could elicit a smile from her son when all she had managed to get in the past few months were assorted grunts, door slammings and general discord.

Someone pushed her from behind and she stumbled into Shad.

"Hey, careful," he warned.

"I *am* being careful," she snapped. "Someone pushed me." She also didn't like the fact that Shad was touching her, holding on to her. The physical contact made her uneasy, edgy, as if she was waiting for something to happen, which was ridiculous. She thought of pulling away, but the crowd wouldn't let her take so much as a step away from him, although she tried.

Shad felt the tension dance between them, as well as the chemistry. He took a quick breath to cut through the snap of desire and released his hold.

J.T. pulled back immediately. "Hey," he warned, grabbing her hand in a deliberately planned, nonchalant movement, "don't hold back. This crowd'll swallow you up. The game's not being broadcast on TV and a lot of people are coming to see it."

Did he think she was an idiot? "I can see that," she muttered between clenched teeth.

Shad decided that J.T.'s problem was that she took everything too seriously. She was simply too uptight. He'd have to see about loosening her up. "Good."

He was smiling patiently and she hated it. This whole evening was going to be an absolutely miserable experience, she could tell. Her hair was coming loose, she was already beginning to perspire in the heat and they hadn't even gotten to their seats yet. Seats? They hadn't even gained access to the entrance yet. J.T. felt herself growing irritable with each step they took.

The sea of people more or less directed their path, and J.T. had the feeling that she wouldn't have been able to turn around now even if she had wanted to. Which she did, but not without her son.

She glanced over toward Francis. She supposed she should be grateful for Shad's presence. At least Francis didn't put up a fuss when Shad took his elbow. J.T. knew that if it had been just the two of them coming here, as unlikely as that seemed, Francis would have never let her hold on to him, and they would have been separated by the heaving crowd, which seemed to have a life of its own.

As the entrance finally loomed before them, a tall, burly man plowed right into J.T., pushing her aside as if she were nothing more than a troublesome insect in his path. J.T. spat out an expletive. Shad laughed in appreciation as he grabbed her arm and pulled her toward him.

So she did have spirit, he thought. He liked that.

She was acutely aware of the fact that she was now pressed up against Shad and her pulse was racing. The intensity of her reaction surprised her. She had thought that part of her long gone. Obviously not. Well, so what? It only proved she was a flesh-and-blood woman. And he was just a man. A man made up of fatty issue and blood vessels and other things best described in a biology book. Telling herself that didn't negate what she was experiencing one iota.

J.T. cleared her throat. "He didn't even realize he walked right into me." She looked accusingly after the man only to discover that she couldn't pick him out. People all around them were grumbling as they sidestepped the threesome. But there was nowhere to go to get out of the way except forward.

"Fanatical fans tend to be oblivious to everything else." Shad looked her over as well as he was able to. The view was limited, but good, infinitely good from where he stood. "Are you all right?"

J.T. turned her head and looked up into Shad's bronzed face. A voice was impatiently calling them to hurry, and J.T. recognized it only vaguely as belonging to her son. What she recognized more accurately was the staccato beating that was going on in her ears. It was her heart.

"Fine," J.T. heard herself mumbling. No, not fine, not fine at all and I don't like it.

"Okay." As if he had been doing this for years, Shad slipped his arm around J.T.'s waist. "If there are no broken bones, let's get out of the way and into the stadium." Taking hold of Frankie's elbow again, Shad hustled them inside.

J.T. had no choice but to keep up with him, ever mindful of the pressure of his hand on her waist. Damn, why didn't he let her go? Because she'd probably be swept away by the tide of humanity, she thought, annoyed that she was temporarily indebted to him. If he hadn't caught her before, she was certain she would have fallen or worse. But it was hard to be grateful to a man she was trying desperately to dislike. What was worse was that she was totally confused as to why she wanted so desperately to dislike him. All she knew was that it had something to do with survival.

Shad gently pressed her back, guiding her and Francis up the flight of stairs. The journey was beginning to seem endless, and she was beginning to feel as if she were part of a stream of human ants, meandering ever onward.

Why was her breathing so labored? She'd gone up stairs before, even winding ones like these. What was it about this man that was disorienting her so? Men had a place in her life. They came holding accounts that needed sorting, companies that needed their finances put to right. They did *not* come in shirts rolled up at the forearms with grins that tingled places that hadn't been tingled in a long time.

She took a deep breath to steady herself and realized they had stopped walking, stopped angling for position, stopped dodging bodies in their quest for the seats that matched their tickets.

"Here?" J.T. was ready to stop just about anywhere at this point as long as she could sit down.

This really was an ordeal for her, Shad thought. Too bad. He could tell that Frankie just reveled in it. "Here." Shad nodded.

J.T. dropped down into the seat. She was still wearing high heels, and the backs of her calves ached, not to mention her toes. She longed to take off her shoes and massage her feet. She wondered how long they'd have to remain here. How long did it usually take for one team to beat the other? She was about to ask, but didn't want to engage Shad in another conversation. It was bad enough that she was forced to sit next to him. He had taken the seat between her and Francis.

The man on her right gave her a curious once-over, and J.T. knew she stood out like a sore thumb. She doubted there was another woman in the stands in heels, a linen skirt and a raw silk blouse that was quickly being ruined.

She was lost in her own thoughts, distantly aware that Francis was still plying Shad with endless questions. Grudgingly she had to admit that he seemed to be answering each one patiently and precisely. He even sounded as if he was enjoying himself, although she couldn't see how.

J.T. rubbed her neck. It was damp. This was what she had wanted, right? To have Francis enjoy himself. So why did she feel so grumpy about it? And so unsettled? Maybe it was just the heat.

Trying to ignore her surroundings and the fact that her clothes were sticking to her, J.T. crossed one leg over the other and, bracing her elbow on her knee, rested her head on her upturned palm to stare at the field. Men in two differently colored uniforms were doing things she had absolutely no interest in.

J.T. felt about as needed and as contented as a bump on a log.

"Hot dog?"

"What?" J.T. turned, her thoughts breaking up and scattering.

"Would you like a hot dog?" Shad pointed to her right. She squinted her eyes against the sun and saw a vendor just coming into view.

"No." The response was automatic. She might have to sit here, broiling in the sun, but she didn't have to put things into her system that were poison.

"She doesn't usually eat meat," Frankie explained. "Says it's not healthy." Frankie's condescending tone gave away his thoughts on the subject.

"I see."

J.T. could have sworn there was a hint of a knowing smile on his face as he said it, even though none was evident to the naked eye. Barbarian. She folded her arms in front of her and stared straight ahead.

"That's probably why you're so skinny."

Her head swung around. "I am not skinny," she retorted defensively.

"Thin, then," Shad corrected himself. To his way of thinking she was a little too thin. It was the kind of thin that came without planning, as if she forgot to eat while she worked. And she probably worked all the time. There were too many people, he thought, who didn't know when to kick back, when to enjoy the fruits of their labors before the season was over and the fruits had dried.

Shad waved and caught the vendor's eye, holding up two fingers. The hot dogs arrived dripping with mustard. Because of her position on the bench, they came to J.T. first. She felt a sudden spasm in her stomach, reminding her that she hadn't eaten dinner. Or lunch.

Her stomach growled, as if to mock her.

Shad inclined his head toward her. "I'll share mine," he offered in a low voice.

She almost said yes. He could see her wavering.

"I won't tell if you don't." He handed Frankie's to him and held up his own in front of J.T. The serpent tempting Eve with the apple.

The rat. He was doing this on purpose. She had half a mind to say no.

Her mind might be saying no, but it was definitely not speaking for her stomach, which persisted in rumbling and embarrassing her. Glaring, she took a bite out of the offered hot dog, then almost sighed. It did taste good. Too good. How could something so bad for you taste so wonderful? She took another bite, intending on giving it back to him after that.

The road to hell was paved with good intentions.

Her eyes met his over the quickly shrinking hot dog. His were laughing. "I can always get another."

J.T. looked down at the hot dog in horror. There was hardly anything left. She thrust it toward him. "I didn't mean to—"

Shad grinned, refusing. He lightly pushed her hand back. "I'm sure you didn't. My treat, remember?" He raised his hand and waved to another vendor. "One thing they never run out of in a stadium is hot dogs."

"Also noise." A wall of din surrounded them, and it was getting louder. "How can you stand it?" She consumed the remainder in one last bite and crumpled up the wax paper, wishing the hot dog had been bigger.

The noise level continued to increase. People all around them were jumping to their feet and cheering. "Now what?" she shouted to Shad.

"The home team just hit a grand slam."

Shad was on his feet, along with Frankie. Before J.T. realized it he had her by the elbow and was coaxing her up, as well. She pulled away and Shad just shrugged carelessly.

He turned and applauded, saying something to Francis that
J.T. didn't catch.

When he turned back, he saw J.T. frowning. He wondered if she was as straitlaced as she seemed, or if something had happened along the way to take all the fun out of
her life. He suspected that it was probably the latter.

"C'mon," he urged, whispering the words into her ear,
"let yourself go."

For a split second the feel of his breath against her skin
blotted out almost everything else. She shook her head to
regain her faculties.

Shad seemed to think it was in answer to him. "Why
not?" He gestured toward the crowd in general. "It's a
healthy release."

J.T. clutched at the offered excuse. She was here, but she
didn't have to like it. "Standing and cheering because the
other team couldn't catch a ball isn't my idea of letting go."

Shad raised an eyebrow, studying her. "Ever try hitting
one over the fence?"

She should have known he'd say something like that.
"No, I—"

"Don't knock it until you do. I'm free next Saturday."

"Good for you." Just what was he getting at?

"We could go and pitch a few."

She had absolutely no intention of seeing this man again.
Especially since a remote part of her actually wanted to.
She'd been in that emotional trap before. "I'm sure you
know just how to pitch, but—"

"Hey," Frankie chimed in excitedly, "that's a great idea!
What time?" He was fairly jumping up and down as they
sat back down on the bench.

Shad considered. "Ten in the morning sound good?"

"Yes!" Frankie cried.

"No," J.T. said firmly.

Shad shrugged good-naturedly. "Okay, I could make it later."

That wasn't what "no" was meant to convey. She was going to have to spell it out for him. "Mr.—"

He placed his hand on her arm and made her skin feel warmer than the sun had. She could have kicked him.

"Shad," he corrected patiently.

She was tempted to wipe that patient expression off his face. He was goading her. "Mr. McClellan," she repeated deliberately, " I assumed this was a onetime deal."

"Dottie wouldn't have felt that it was," Shad pointed out. Frankie grinned broadly.

J.T. tried to ignore her son. "You're planning on taking her place?"

"Until she's well enough to come herself, yes. I made her a promise." Well, all right, he thought, that was stretching it. But there was no one to catch him in the lie.

Maybe keeping his word meant something to him, and maybe it was something else. J.T. didn't know. She did know that she just wasn't up to this kind of ordeal more than once. "I really don't—"

"Want to make any hasty decisions. I understand. We'll discuss it after the game."

He had the most infuriating habit of ending her sentences for her with the exact opposite meaning from what she'd intended. There was no point in arguing about it now. Francis looked as if he was hanging on every one of this man's words, and J.T. didn't want to ruin the game for him. Besides, she knew what she was going to do, whatever was on Shad's mind.

"All right," J.T. agreed. "We'll discuss it after the game." And then I'll say no, J.T. thought.

Chapter Three

"Catch it, Mom. Catch it!"

Francis's urgent scream penetrated J.T.'s consciousness just as something whizzed by her head, hit the metal railing directly behind her, bounced off her shoulder and then neatly came to rest in her skirt.

J.T. stifled a gasp as she stared at the baseball in her lap, stunned. A chorus of disappointed groans met her ears. Eager fans dropped outstretched hands and sat down again to watch the rest of the game.

"You got it!" Frankie stamped his feet and cheered.

"It's a baseball," J.T. cried incredulously.

"There are a lot of those around here." Shad grinned, amused. "Nice catch." He saw the slightly dazed look on J.T.'s face. The ball probably couldn't have done much damage, but pain was a relative thing. "Are you hurt?" He ran the back of his fingertips over the area of her shoulder where the ball had hit.

J.T. tried not to wince. "Only when I breathe."

Her bone structure was fragile, Shad judged, suddenly concerned. "Can you move it?"

Because he was obviously waiting for a demonstration, J.T. rotated her shoulder with slow, tentative movements. Her damp blouse felt clammy against her skin, and a warm ache fanned out from the point of impact. "Yes."

Her eyes misted slightly. He bet it hurt like hell. "Then it's not broken."

"I know that," she said defensively. If he thought she was trying for sympathy—

"Want to have it looked at?"

It was a way to free her from this purgatory she found herself in, J.T. thought, but that would mean dragging her son away from the game, and this was practically the first time in months she and Francis had occupied the same space for more than five minutes without heated words passing between them. She'd put up with a little pain in exchange for that. A little pain and a tall one with very soulful eyes.

J.T. shook her head. "No, I'll live."

Amusement softened the hard lines of his face. "Some of us are relieved to hear that." Shad put his hand out, unwilling to take the ball from her until she offered it. "May I?"

J.T. shrugged. "Sure." With a small flip of her wrist she passed the ball to him.

Frankie craned his neck around Shad, all but drooling as he looked at the ball wistfully. "Wow."

J.T. hadn't seen Francis like this in quite a while. Most of the time Francis was trying too hard to be the disinterested preteen. Eagerness was something J.T. could relate to, even if it involved a ball.

"Do you want it?" It was beyond J.T. why anyone would regard this rather dirty-looking ball as something special. All baseballs looked alike, didn't they? She had seen Francis handle baseballs countless times. But the look in Francis's eyes told her that obviously her son didn't see things quite that way.

Frankie looked up almost hesitantly at his mother, apparently forgetting that a schism existed between them. "Can I? Can I really have it?"

J.T. was at a loss as to how to react to this almost worshipful, timid question coming from her flippant son. A pleased feeling filtered through. "I don't see why not." She watched Shad hand it over to Francis, who took it reverently into his hands.

"I could get that autographed for you," Shad volunteered after a moment.

"You could?" Frankie's eyes were wide.

"Sure." His tone was matter-of-fact, but he couldn't hide the satisfaction he was experiencing from his face. He was enjoying this. "I know a couple of the players."

"Personally?" Frankie breathed.

Shad felt J.T.'s eyes burning into the back of his neck and wondered why his simple offer was annoying her. Maybe he shouldn't have said anything. Still, he knew that an autographed ball was a bigger treasure than an unautographed one. "Personally."

"Here." Frankie thrust the ball at him.

"You hang on to it until after the game."

Obediently Francis willingly did as he was told. J.T. could only marvel at the transformation. She let out a breath and felt it almost hang in the air in front of her. God, she was hot. The heat felt as if it would never subside. She looked up absently at the sky.

Shad raised his eyes upward. There was nothing to see. "What are you looking for?"

Defiantly J.T. kept on looking. The sun was turning crimson. "I'm checking to see if there are any vultures circling around yet."

"Vultures?"

"Sure." She looked at him. "They must know that in this heat there are bound to be people roasting to death."

He laughed. Her tongue was sharp, but he kind of liked that. "I take it you're hot."

"You're very perceptive for a kidnapper."

His eyebrows drew together, bemused. "I didn't kidnap you."

"You lured my son here with baseball tickets." She saw traces of a grin form at the corners of his mouth, and she deliberately shut out the reaction that created. Or thought she did. "I couldn't very well let him go off alone."

"No," he agreed, "you couldn't."

If she didn't know any better, she would have said he had planned it this way, inviting Francis out, knowing she'd have to come along, too. But that was ridiculous because he hadn't even seen her until he appeared on their doorstep.

Her head began to ache. It was the heat. And the noise. And the company.

To block out the latter J.T. stared down at the field. She watched as a batter swung and missed twice, then sent a ball flying back over the foul line. It was retrieved and the batter stayed where he was. J.T. frowned. Something didn't seem right.

Shad noticed her expression. "What's the matter?"

"Why isn't he out?" J.T. asked.

"Who?"

"The player down there." She pointed vaguely in the direction of the field. "That was his third swing, right?"

"Yes."

"Well, isn't he out then?"

Shad began to answer her, then stopped. He glanced to his right. "Frankie?"

J.T. noticed that the boy seemed to come to life at the sound of Shad's voice. They'd known him how long? An hour? Why couldn't she get a response like that? Other than when she was handing the boy a dirty, worn ball of course.

"Yes?" Francis transferred the baseball from one hand to the other, then back again, his fingers caressing the ball at each pass. J.T. had thought those fingers suited to playing the piano, just as she had. Francis had thought otherwise.

"Your mom's got a question about the game. Do you want to answer it?"

"Well, it really wasn't a question—" J.T. started. She didn't actually care if the man was out or not; she just had a vague impression he was supposed to be if he hit a foul ball. Maybe they had changed the rules. It was a long way back to those Sunday afternoons when her father used to watch the games in his den. She remembered listening to them, wishing she could enter the dark, cool den with him, wishing she could share something with him. But that was his time to relax, and she hadn't been allowed to be part of it. Children had their place in the Trent household.

Shad gave J.T. a warning look, moving his head from side to side ever so slightly. Her protest halted in midsentence. What was he up to?

Francis shrugged, but J.T. could tell he was pleased by the display of interest. "Sure. It's 'cause he's already got two strikes."

That didn't make any sense. "And?" J.T. prodded, looking back at the field. The player hit a grounder to third and was pronounced safe at first.

"If he hits a foul ball after the second time and nobody catches it, it's not counted as anything."

J.T. curbed the urge to say that that was a dumb rule. Obviously it wasn't to Francis. "Oh," she mumbled.

Shad leaned toward her. "It'll grow on you," he promised.

She wished he wouldn't sit so closely. "Not if I can help it." *And that goes for you, too, no matter what you've got on your mind.*

It occurred gradually. One moment she was staring off into space, silently bemoaning this waste of time, and then slowly, without being conscious of it, her line of vision shifted to the field for lack of anything else to hold her attention. That was when it happened. She started watching. Out of boredom at first. Then out of curiosity. It didn't hurt matters any that the sun was going down and the evening breeze had lifted, cooling everything off.

Shad noted the shift in her body language. It went from ramrod straight to a relaxed, fluid position as J.T. leaned her elbow on her crossed legs and watched. He was tempted to comment but had a hunch she wouldn't appreciate an "I told you so" at this point.

Maybe later, after he had really gotten to know the lady. And he would get to know her.

As J.T. watched the game, she found that more and more things needed explaining. But each time she asked Shad about something, he deliberately turned to Francis. J.T. was surprised at the amount of information her son had compiled in his head. She was equally surprised that Shad was apparently considerate enough to let him share it. Most men would have tried to steal the spotlight.

J.T. looked at him thoughtfully.

People around them began gathering their things together and rising as the Angels poured out of their dugout, slapping one another on the back. Fascinated, J.T. remained motionless, watching. Shad leaned over toward her. "It's over," he whispered.

"No, it's not," she insisted. To verify her statement she looked over at the scoreboard. The bottom of the ninth's space was empty. "They have a half inning to play." Because everyone else was now up, J.T. rose to her feet, but stayed where she was.

"There's no point," Shad explained, placing his body so that J.T. didn't see the smirk on Frankie's face. There was a lot to be worked out here, he thought. "The home team would be going into the bottom of the ninth with a two-point lead. The only thing that could happen would be an even bigger spread in the score."

"If you ask me," J.T. mumbled to herself, taking her purse, "there's no point to the whole game." Her comment earned her a surprised and sullen look from Francis. It was the expression he usually wore.

Shad caught the exchange between mother and son. This, he thought, was what his partner Angelo's father had always referred to as the generation gap. Angelo's father's way of handling it was an affectionate but none-too-gentle cuff on the ear. He didn't think that was going to solve very much in this case.

Shad placed his hand on the back of J.T.'s neck. It was a gesture, J.T. thought, that was much too possessive. For the time being, because she'd probably be engulfed by the crowd and lose track of Francis if she pulled away, she let Shad's hand stay where it was.

He couldn't resist. "Why, J.T., don't tell me you didn't enjoy yourself tonight."

She started to say that was *exactly* what she was going to tell him, but then she stopped. Honesty kept her from it. Reviewing the evening in her mind, it would have been a lie to deny that she'd had a reasonably good time. She'd spent worse. Going over Grimes's account, for instance, which would have been the way she would have spent the evening had she not been whisked away. The evening would have been productive then, not to mention financially rewarding. But enjoyable? No. Not by any stretch of the imagination could she have called it that. Besides, just watching Francis have a good time made it all worthwhile.

"I've spent worse evenings," she allowed.

Shad laughed as they melded into the line of people funneling down the stairway. "Your mother isn't given to overstatements, is she?"

Frankie, still clutching his ball, shook his head.

"Well, I think an evening where you've learned a few things is always enjoyable." He saw an opening and guided Frankie through it, carefully staying behind him and keeping J.T. at his side. "Are you two ready to call it an evening?"

"Yes," J.T. said quickly with a rush of relief.

Frankie swung around on the stairs, bumping into the woman in front of him. "No."

"There seems to be a slight difference of opinion here." He could almost hear what J.T. was thinking. "Calls for a compromise, as I see it."

Enough was enough. "I don't care how you see—" J.T. began.

"What sort of a compromise?" Frankie asked eagerly.

It seemed to be J.T.'s day for not getting sentences out.

Shad pointed in front of him, and Frankie obediently continued walking. "I was thinking along the lines of getting some ice cream at the mall by your house. How does that sound?''

J.T. wanted to say no. She was going to say no. How the word turned into yes on the tip of her tongue she had absolutely no idea. Magic, she supposed. Or the product of an exhausted woman who'd had a ball thrown at her. ''Why not?''

His resonant laugh engulfed her far more fully than the crowd. ''I'll take that as a resounding yes, but you're going to have to learn how to curb your enthusiasm.''

What I'd like to curb, J.T. thought, is you.

She wasn't prepared for the quick, one-armed hug he gave her and consequently reacted to it before she suddenly pulled away, annoyed at him for taking advantage.

The lady, he thought, obviously didn't trust men. He knew he'd have to find out why before he could get any farther.

J.T. had never been inside the mall's ice-cream parlor, with its old-fashioned wrought-iron tables and chairs. Since she had moved here her life had just been too busy for carefree afternoons where she could allow herself the luxury of just relaxing. She always had to have a purpose, a focus. This was something new.

''What flavor of ice cream?'' Shad asked, noting the way J.T. was absorbing it all. Obviously she didn't come here often, he decided.

''Yogurt,'' J.T. corrected.

''I might have known.''

She didn't like the way he was pigeonholing her. ''Low-cal. Strawberry,'' she said in short, clip words.

Shad looked at the young woman in the pink-and-white uniform behind the counter. ''You heard the lady. I'll take a double scoop of rum raisin.''

"Me, too," Frankie echoed.

"Make that two." He turned toward J.T. "Sure you won't change your mind?"

J.T. pressed her lips together firmly. "I'm sure."

Don't be, he thought.

They found a table, and J.T. sat and slowly ate her yogurt while Frankie and Shad discussed the highlights of the evening's ball game, team standings in general and the Angels' chances of actually winning the pennant that year. Throughout it all Shad watched her. Even when he seemed to be devoting his full attention to Frankie, he watched her. And J.T. knew it.

"You do everything that methodically?" he finally asked.

J.T. looked up slowly from her dish. She didn't like looking into his eyes. But there was no avoiding it. They made her feel vulnerable, as if she was wearing the wrong clothes or had forgotten something. As if she was that woman she tried so hard to bury. "What?"

"You're eating that yogurt as if you were following written instructions. First the right side, then the left, then the right, then the left. Have you ever felt like cutting loose and attacking the top first?"

Frankie laughed.

J.T. put her spoon down. "I'm enjoying it."

"Are you?"

What was it about this man that seemed to challenge her with a look, a nuance? Why did she feel as if she couldn't hide things from him?

"Of course I am," she insisted a bit too forcefully. She threw her napkin onto the table. "I think we should be getting home now, unless, of course, you have a tour of Disneyland in mind."

Her sarcasm left him unruffled. "Not a bad idea. Maybe next time."

"Next time?" J.T. echoed in surprise.

"Dottie won't be on her feet for about six weeks, although knowing her, she's probably trying to hobble out of the hospital even as we speak. Anyway, until she's ready I thought—"

She knew what he was about to say and she didn't want to hear it. "You thought incorrectly, Mr. McClellan."

He would have needed an ice pick to chip off the frost that encased his name. "Back to first base?"

"Back to the dugout," she corrected. She realized that for whatever reason, her response sounded too intense. It *was* too intense. All right, she wasn't being fair. "Look, I appreciate what you did tonight—"

"I didn't *do* anything." He saw the way Frankie was paying attention to the exchange and knew he'd have to word things carefully. The foster home he had spent half his formative years in had been filled with warmth and love. He thought everyone's should be. "You caught the ball."

What was he getting at now? "Are you deliberately trying to confuse me?"

"Could be. How am I doing?"

J.T. shut her eyes, gathering her thoughts together and searching for strength.

Shad turned to Frankie. "Is she meditating?"

Frankie laughed.

J.T.'s eyes opened. There was an impatient, exasperated look in them. "No, 'she's' struggling to find the words to tell you that it's over—"

"But it hasn't even begun. Yet."

She wondered what Francis would say if he saw his mother hit a man in an ice-cream parlor. "Why are you doing this?"

"Maybe because I enjoy the company. Maybe because it was a fun evening."

He helped her with her chair. It was either get up or fall off. J.T. got up.

Shad grinned. "Maybe because I like checked floors in old-fashioned ice-cream parlors."

Francis, J.T. could tell, was willing to accept any one of these insane explanations. She, however, wasn't. What was this man's angle? Why was he so eager to shoehorn his way into their lives?

Bedeviled, J.T. took the offensive. "I'd appreciate it if you took us home, Mr. McClellan."

He held the front door open for them. The bell that was mounted above it tinkled lightly. "That was part of the deal."

J.T. passed through, keeping as far away from him as physically possible. "What deal?"

He winked. "I'll fill you in as we go along."

In a moment of mounting fear and exasperation J.T. began to wonder how they were going to get rid of this man once he brought them home. *If* he brought them home.

She hesitated at the door of his car, and he could almost read what was on her mind. "Don't worry," he assured her quietly. "There's nothing else on tonight's agenda." His tone lightened again. "Unless, of course, you'd like to invite me in."

"I wouldn't."

"Well," he considered the matter philosophically, "then I guess there isn't anything left except to deliver you safely to your doorstep." He closed the passenger door and crossed to the driver's side.

"Are you really going to get my ball autographed for me?" Frankie asked.

Shad got in, then grinned at Frankie. "Absolutely."

He was filling her son's head with promises, J.T. thought. Promises he'd probably forget to keep. She didn't want that to happen. Not again. Pete had done things like that. Promised to come and visit Francis. The boy had stood by the door waiting for hours, dressed and ready and hopeful. And he never came. J.T. didn't want that kind of hurt dug up again.

"Just who is it that you know on the team?" J.T. asked pointedly as Shad brought his car to a stop next to hers in her driveway. She didn't know the name of a single man on the team, but she was sure Francis did.

Shad suspected that J.T. thought he was simply bragging. He supposed he couldn't blame her. He gave her three names for good measure, though there were more that he knew. They were all resident Californians, men whose homes he had worked on in the past four years, starting with the manager.

Frankie's eyes threatened to fall out. "Really?"

"I'll have them autograph it for you by next week," he promised. Sooner if he could help it.

J.T. got out of the car and slammed the door. "Let's go Francis. You still have some homework to do." It was a lucky guess. Francis *always* had homework left to do.

"Oh, Mom." Frankie moaned. Sullenly he shuffled over to the front door. There, he turned and waved. "Bye. Shad."

"Bye. I'll see you soon."

Not if I can help it, J.T. thought.

Shad hung back just a little, walking behind J.T. "You'r being prejudiced, you know," he told her softly, his hand on her shoulder.

She felt a slight jolt when he touched her. Why did he persist in doing that? Touching her, scrambling her thoughts. J.T. whirled around, surprised at his statement. "What?"

Why was she so rigid? He'd done nothing to provoke it. He pretended not to notice that she had shrugged off his hand. "You would have never treated my sister this way."

No, and his sister wouldn't have made her feel this way, either. She didn't like this tension, this sizzle in the air. Excitement and anticipation only led to disappointment. She had too much going on in her life, had crafted her life too carefully, to allow this sort of thing to seep through the cracks.

She didn't appear to have a say in the matter.

But she could bar him from her life.

"No," J.T. agreed. "I wouldn't. Good night, Mr. McClellan."

He saluted. J.T. turned her back on him. She could almost feel him grinning as she stepped inside and closed the door behind her. He was infuriating and tempting, and she detested him for it. J.T. consoled herself with the fact that at least she had seen the last of him.

Chapter Four

"Well, I thought he was neat," Frankie declared loudly over the mandatory glass of milk he hated.

J.T. raised her eyes from her plate. The defiant look on her son's face didn't surprise her. J.T. sighed. How could she make him understand? "You're young yet."

She could feel the tension building. Arguing with Francis always made her lose her appetite. It was wonderful for her figure but very hard on her nerves. She had made a special effort to be home for dinner tonight. It didn't require a trained child psychologist, like the one who hadn't shown up, to interpret her reactions. It was obvious, even though J.T. didn't want to admit it, that she was competing with Shad.

But all she and Francis had managed to do from the moment she had walked through the front door was argue. As usual. The topic might be different—the charismatic stranger who had shown up in his sister's place—but the lines that were drawn were unaltered. Lately they were always the same. And firmly imprinted. Righteous teen versus horrid mother. It was getting very, very old.

"What does that have to do with it?" Frankie demanded. He frowned as he played with the food on his plate.

J.T. eyed her son's untouched meal and guessed that an afternoon binge on junk food was the reason for his abstinence. "You're too trusting."

"You got into his car, too." Frankie stuck out his chin.

That wasn't what she was referring to, but J.T. let it go. "Maybe I'm too trusting. The point is, that although we had a rather nice evening," she said, enunciating the words as if they were being pulled out of her against her will, "we won't be seeing Mr. McClellan again."

She didn't need that kind of distraction in her life. Lately, with everything pulling at her from all directions, it was hard to cope. The demands at work were mounting, and Francis was getting farther and farther away from her. The last thing she needed was a pushy man who disoriented her. And made her remember.

Frankie formed his mashed potatoes into a mound with his fork. "Yes, we will. He promised to bring back my ball. Autographed."

J.T. doubted the man even remembered he had the baseball, much less made the promise. "We'll see. Please stop playing with your food, Francis."

Frankie scowled at the use of his name. "And he gave you his number," he reminded her. "In case you needed it."

That was just the way Shad had worded it when he had given his number to her at the ball game. *In case she needed it.* What on earth made him think she would need it, or him? "I threw it out."

"You threw it out?" Frankie cried. "When?"

"Last night when I was cleaning out my purse in the den." Why was he so upset? He hardly knew the man. "Francis, I—"

"Why?" There was obvious pain and a sense of betrayal in the single word.

J.T. hated being challenged over every action, every word. Why couldn't Francis just accept things once in a while? Her son's reaction made her feel suddenly very tired. "Because we don't need it. Because I always throw out useless clutter."

It was her way of dealing with life. Once, she had been a romantic, collecting mementos from every event that carried any significance, however small. Once, she thought ruefully, she had been a wide-eyed fool. All the junk, all the memorabilia, had gone into the trash the day she divorced Pete. Along with her useless dreams.

"But I thought—" Frankie stopped, pouting as he stared down at the tablecloth. His hair fell into his eyes.

J.T. put down her fork. There was no use in pretending she was going to eat. "You thought what?" J.T. prodded, trying to keep her voice calm. When Francis raised his head, J.T. saw the veil that had fallen over his eyes.

"I thought I'd call him or something," he mumbled.

J.T. looked at him sharply. "Why?"

Frankie shrugged defensively. "I've got this science project coming up. I thought he might help." His voice trailed off. He turned his face away and looked out the dining room window.

J.T. hated seeing Francis like this, hated the wall that had gone up between them. Science was a subject J.T. knew very little about and liked even less. Maybe they'd muddle through it together. "I'll help."

Frankie turned to look at her. His expression was old, mocking. "When? Sandwiched in between accounts?"

Benevolent feelings faded as J.T. lost her patience. "Francis, I'll thank you to change your tone of voice. I'm not doing this for recreation. I'm earning a living, in case you haven't noticed. I—"

The cynical look in Francis's eyes stopped her. Oh, what was the use? It seemed that since the beginning of the year, Francis refused to understand anything that had to do with his mother's life. How different they were, she and her son. When she had been a child, she had understood. She understood the limitations her parents had put on her, understood that there were things she had no power over. She had accepted things.

And dreamed of something better, richer. Warmer.

Well, hadn't that ultimately been the problem? The world she had grown up in hadn't taught her how to see the real world. And that was why Pete had managed to sweep her off her feet the way he had. Because she had been grounded in a fantasy world, not life. He had said he loved her, and she had sold her soul for the simple phrase.

"Seems to me it wouldn't hurt having that man over for dinner maybe." The swinging kitchen door creaked as it shut behind Norma.

J.T. was startled by the unexpected comment from her housekeeper. The man had defenders coming out of the woodwork. "And just when did you get a chance to see him, Norma? As I recall, you were glued to your set in the kitchen."

"They have commercials," Norma answered pointedly with a knowing smile. She set out the two dishes of chocolate mousse she had brought in. "He was kind of cute. Like that guy on that Western Saturday nights."

J.T. picked up a spoon, but had little intention of eating. Nothing seemed to taste right anymore. "Does everything relate back to television for you, Norma?"

Norma frowned over the two dinners that had barely been touched. She picked up one plate, scraped it off onto the other and then stacked the two together. Her soft, angelically round face looked philosophical as she glanced J.T.'s way. "Art imitates life."

J.T. wasn't in the mood to debate with another member of her household. Why did everyone act as if Shad McClellan was someone sent from heaven? They didn't even know this man. "Very profound, Norma. Ever watch *The Boston Strangler?*"

Norma shook her head as she picked up the two plates, the point J.T. was trying to make lost on her. "He doesn't look a thing like Tony Curtis." The shine in her eyes showed there was a lot more to Norma than just work and television. "Too well built."

J.T. gave up. She was outnumbered. For whatever reason, Shadrach McClellan had obviously impressed both her housekeeper and her son. But she still made the rules.

"Now hear this, you two. Mr. McClellan isn't being invited back even if he looked like Mel Gibson." She rose. "No dessert for me tonight, Norma." With that, she left the room, heading for the staircase and a change of clothes.

Norma watched her go, shaking her head. She let out a large, judgmental sigh before looking at Frankie. "That's what happens to a woman when she works as hard as your mother. She loses perspective." Using her back, Norma pushed open the door to the kitchen. In the background the theme song of yet another family comedy, gone into reruns, was playing. Norma moved faster. "I'd save that number from the trash if I were you," she said without looking over her shoulder.

Frankie scrambled out of his chair and headed for the den.

* * *

Shad rocked in his chair, his back to the drawing board that held the plans of his company's latest construction site. There were blueprints to look over one last time and a bid to finalize. His mind wasn't on it. Instead, with his feet propped on his desk, he sat passing Frankie's baseball from hand to hand, staring out the window. His mind was in the past. Twenty-four hours in the past. She had been preying on his mind like a haunting melody that refused to end. He scarcely heard the door behind him open and then close again.

"I thought you'd gone home." Angelo Marino crossed the room in large, well-measured strides, creating an image of a man far bigger than he actually was. People always remembered him as taller, wider. Impressive. There were touches of premature gray nipping at the sides of his temples and shooting through his thick head of jet-black hair. Five-ten, brawny, at thirty-six he was the spitting image of his father, the man who had taken both Shad and Dottie in so many years ago.

Angelo nodded at the baseball in Shad's hand. "What's that?"

Shad glanced up. Images of J.T.'s mouth, soft and supple, faded. He laughed. "You mean a man your age doesn't recognize a baseball, Angie?"

Angelo sat on the edge of his foster brother's desk. A thick, wide hand grabbed the ball easily in midpass and held it.

"A man my age recognizes daydreaming when he sees it." Angelo examined the ball for a moment, then raised his eyes to Shad. "Okay, what gives?"

Shad dropped his feet from the desk and sat up in his chair. "I'm not sure."

"Always an encouraging statement coming from your partner upon whom half your livelihood is riding." Angelo threw the ball up and caught it before he went on. "Trouble?" He glanced over toward the drawing board. Several drawings were tacked on, but nothing seemed out of order.

"No," Shad answered slowly, still thinking, "not the way you mean."

Angelo grinned. The expression was lopsided and made him look like a boy despite the touch of gray. "Oh. That way."

Shad shook his head. It had always been so simple for him before. Somehow this wasn't simple. Not the lady, not the feeling. "Not quite."

"Meaning?"

"The lady is made of ice."

Angelo hopped off the desk, tossing the ball back to Shad. "Never knew that to be a problem for you. Hey." He gave Shad's shoulder an affectionate swat. "You remember what Pop always said?" He became more animated, using his hands as he spoke the way his father had. "You see something you like, you go after it. You give it a try. Who knows?" His wide, powerful shoulders lifted and fell again. "It might even work out."

Shad shook off his pensive mood. "Words to live by."

"I always found them to be." Angelo glanced over toward the bulletin board next to the window. It was covered with order forms and schedules, a sure sign their business was thriving. "Meanwhile, why don't you give Kennedy a call for me? He was supposed to have that tile delivered at the Taffin Restaurant this morning. Allan Taffin is fit to be tied."

"No tile?"

"No tile."

Shad reached for his card file and began thumbing through it for their supplier's phone number. "Damn."

"That about describes it." Angelo turned to go out the door, then swung around on his heel. "Oh, you bringing Dottie home tonight?"

Shad nodded absently, still looking for the number. "It's either that or she'll be tying sheets together and lowering herself out the hospital window."

Angelo laughed. It was a booming laugh that filled the room. "I can see her doing that."

"Yeah, so can I. Got it." Shad pulled out Kennedy's number. Just as he reached for the phone, it rang.

"Answer that, will you?" Angelo said. "I promised Ma I'd come over for dinner tonight. If I'm late, she'll kill me."

"Better you than me. Last time I ate there I couldn't close my pants when I left." Angelo closed the door and Shad picked up the receiver. "Hello, Marino and McClellan."

"Is...is Shad there?" the young voice asked uncertainly.

It took him only a moment to connect the voice with a face. "Frankie?" He immediately straightened up, alert. Had his mother asked him to call?

There was an audible sigh of relief on the other end. "Yeah. I was afraid you might have forgotten."

"No chance." He glanced at the baseball on his desk. It now bore the signatures of three of the Angels. It made for quite a trophy, he thought. "I've got the ball right here." He started to reach for it.

"Oh, right, the ball."

He thought it odd that Frankie would have forgotten about it. Was he trying to be nonchalant, or was there was another reason why he was calling? He left the ball where it was. "Is anything wrong, Frankie?"

"No, it's just that, well, I've got this science project coming up and I really need help with it," Frankie said, ending his sentence in a rush.

He thought back to the science projects he had made when he was a boy. He and Salvator had worked on them for hours on the dining room table. Remembering made him smile. "Have you asked your mother?"

"Yeah. She said she'd help."

There was no mistaking the disappointment in the boy's voice. "But?"

"She'll probably forget."

"Give her a chance, Frankie. She's a busy lady."

"Yeah, well, she's also lousy in science. She even said so once. Could you maybe—?" Frankie's voice drifted off, hesitant.

Shad recognized the fear of being rejected when he heard it. He had lived with it himself as a child. "Help?" he supplied.

"Yes."

Shad glanced at his calendar. It didn't look any different than it did every other week. It was full. But he could always make time. He had made it a point in his life that there would always be time to stop and be human. Besides, how could he say no when Frankie sounded so hopeful? He wondered how J.T. could turn her back on that, work or no work. He remembered that he had offered to come by on Saturday. So be it. With a little bit of effort it could be managed. "Saturday okay?"

"Saturday's great." He could hear the smile in Frankie's voice.

"Will your mother be there?"

"Why?"

"Just wondering. Maybe she'd like to get involved."

"I don't think so. But she'll probably be in and out," Frankie answered. "Saturdays she only spends half her time in the office. But Norma's always around."

He was right. Ms. J. T. Mayne was a workaholic. She needed to be shown the finer things in life. And he was just the one to show her. "Norma?"

"Our housekeeper."

"Then it's a date, as long as you clear it with your mother."

"Do I have to?"

He laughed at the pain attached to Frankie's response. "'Fraid so."

Frankie groaned.

"Frankie, I got the definite impression that your mother isn't too crazy about me. I wouldn't want to stroll into her house without her permission." Except as a last resort, he added silently.

"It's not you. She's not too crazy about men in general."

"Doesn't date?" The question slipped out before he thought it through, but now that it was out he waited for the answer.

"I've never seen a guy here. I don't think she has time."

"Well, we'll just have to see that she makes time—for everything," he added. "Did you have a project in mind?"

"I dunno. Maybe something about space?"

"Okay, I'll see what I can come up with. Now promise you'll ask her if Saturday's all right."

Frankie sighed deeply. "All right, I promise. Bye."

As Shad hung up the phone, he wondered if Frankie would actually keep his word. He thought of calling J.T. himself, then stopped. Frankie wouldn't appreciate being checked up on. He had promised and he would have to give the boy a chance to live up to his word. Besides, he did want

to see them again. Both of them. He liked Frankie, and as
for J.T., well, he had been truthful with Angelo when he
said he didn't know. But he did know he wanted to explore
this further, see what the lady was made of. See why he was
so attracted to her when she kept giving off signals that said
she definitely wasn't interested. Maybe it was just the challenge.

Or maybe it was the lure of the family situation. He'd
just have to see.

Frankie had said that J.T. was in and out on Saturday.
He'd check for her car when he drove up to make sure she
was in when he arrived. Maybe, he mused, linking his
hands behind his head as he leaned back in his chair, he
might even convince her to stay.

The baseball on his desk caught his eye, and he remembered the way J.T. had looked when it had landed in her
lap. Her eyes had opened wide in stunned surprise. He
wondered if they'd open that way when he kissed her. Or
would she close them, allowing her mind to drift? He made
himself a promise to find out as soon as possible. His own,
he knew, would close. It heightened the enjoyment.

"I don't see why I can't just go to my own apartment,
Shad," Dottie protested as she hobbled into the house on
crutches, her right leg encased in a full-length cast that in
the space of a little more than twenty-four hours had been
almost completely covered with signatures.

Shad walked in behind her, cutting his long stride in order not to bump into her. She hadn't mastered moving
around on crutches yet. In his hands he carried the two
suitcases of clothes that Angelo had hastily packed for
Dottie earlier that evening. He deposited them just inside
the guest bedroom before he answered her.

Crossing back into the living room, he shoved his hands into his back pockets. "Dottie, it was either staying with me or with Ma. And you know how she can fuss."

Dottie closed her eyes, thinking of her foster mother. The woman was seventy and still cooked a mean seven-course meal every Sunday for all the relatives she could browbeat into attending. Dottie loved the woman dearly, but she knew she'd go out of her mind inside of a few days, being hovered over. "You saved me from that?"

"That and gaining twenty pounds before you finished convalescing."

Dottie glanced at the remains of that evening's TV dinner on the coffee table. In his haste to pick her up Shad had forgotten to throw it out.

"Not much chance of that happening here," Dottie said cheerfully. With care she positioned herself in front of the navy blue leather recliner. Shad moved behind her, ready to help. "I'm not a baby, Shad," Dottie snapped and immediately regretted it. She shook her head twice, the swirls of strawberry-blond hair bouncing against her face and shoulders. "Sorry. This 'inconvenience' just has me testy."

"Really?" He raised his eyebrows. "I didn't notice any difference."

"Thanks a lot." Shad took the crutches from her and watched as she lowered herself onto the recliner, gripping the armrests tightly until she was seated. Dottie let out a breath. "How did it go with Frankie last night? Was he very disappointed? You didn't give me many details."

"That's because you were too busy complaining about having to stay overnight in the hospital." He set her crutches down next to the recliner. "It went fine. I'm helping Frankie with his science project Saturday." He tossed Dottie the remote control for the television.

Dottie frowned as she caught it. Impatiently she tapped her cast. "Maybe I can go there and—"

"No, you're going to rest."

Dottie looked at him accusingly. "You promised not to fuss."

Shad backed up, his hands raised. "That's not fussing. That's keeping you from running off before you're able. One trip to the hospital is all I can handle, okay? Besides, I kind of like helping out."

Dottie raised her eyebrows. "Oh?" There was anticipation in her voice.

"Yes." Deliberately he avoided her eyes. He knew she was consumed by curiosity and he liked teasing her. "It gives me a good feeling to share some of my time with someone who's deserving."

"Frankie's only twelve."

"Yes." Shad propped a pillow behind her back. "But his mother's about thirty-two."

Dottie craned her neck to catch sight of his expression. "Pretty?"

"Yes, in a reserved sort of way." Then, because he had shared almost everything with Dottie, he went on. "I got her to go to the baseball game with us."

"You went to the game?"

"I hated to waste the tickets, especially since you bought three."

Dottie winced at the reminder. "Habit. I'm used to buying tickets for you, Angelo and me. But you said you were just going to go to apologize because I couldn't make it," she reminded him.

Shad shrugged. "I got carried away."

"So I see." A strong family resemblance was evident in the wide, pleased smile that took hold of her lips and highlighted her eyes.

Shad tweaked her nose. "Smirking doesn't become you, little sister."

Dottie rubbed her nose with the back of her hand. "Sorry."

He doubted it. "That's better." It was almost ten o'clock and he was tired, but there was still one more errand to run. "I'd better get those animals of yours over here."

"Then you didn't forget." When he talked her into staying with him earlier today, he had promised to bring her pets over, as well. Since they hadn't come running to the door just now, she thought he had forgotten. She should have known better. Shad never forgot anything.

"No, but I would have liked to," he said with a sigh as he went to the front door. "See you in about half an hour."

"Thanks."

Shad glanced over his shoulder. Dottie had cocked her head and was watching him thoughtfully. He ignored her and left.

Chapter Five

"You did what?"

J.T. all but sputtered as she stared at Francis across from her at the dining room table. Her eyes narrowed as she replayed her son's words in her head.

"I called Shad and asked him to come over Saturday to help me with my science project." Stubborn blue eyes challenged her. "He said okay."

"But you can't just ask a strange man to the house like that." J.T. watched as Francis jabbed defiantly at his asparagus. The fork hit the plate, scraping down the length of it. The noise set J.T.'s teeth on edge.

"He's not a strange man," Frankie insisted. "We went to the ball game with him."

"That's not exactly something we can use as a character reference." She didn't like the idea that Shad had agreed to see Francis without calling her first and clearing it. Just who did he think he was?

That was exactly what she wasn't planning to find out, she reminded herself. Under no circumstances was that man setting foot inside her house again. Once was more than enough.

"Huh?" Frankie looked at her blankly.

"Francis." J.T. saw the annoyed look on the young face deepen. "Frankie," she amended with a restrained sigh. "We just can't ask him over."

"*We* didn't. *I* did."

He was playing with words. Francis had been difficult about so many things these past few months. Why should this be any different? J.T. thought in despair. A dozen articles she had read in the papers whizzed through J.T.'s mind at once. Stories about children being abducted because they stopped to talk to a stranger. Stories about children going off to school and never being seen again. What if Shad was really one of those types of men, just biding his time? If anything ever happened to Francis, she would never forgive herself. She had to protect him.

Despite his bravado, Francis was as naive as a twelve-year-old had a right to be. J.T. wished she was that innocent again, that trusting. She had been once. But the world with its sharp edges had intruded, and she knew things weren't that simple anymore. They never had been. Idyllic friendships were few and far between and selfless people even fewer.

But how did she explain this to Francis? Simple, she didn't. There was no way to make him understand. He was too stubborn to hear. But J.T. loved her son far too much to risk anything happening to him just to placate the boy.

"Fine. And *I'll* cancel it." J.T. held out her hand expectantly. "Where's his number?"

Frankie shrugged. "I dunno."

"Francis." J.T.'s voice was soft, measured, but there was no mistaking the warning note. Grumbling, the boy dug the number out of the pocket of his jeans and handed it to her. "Why didn't you ask me before you called him?" she asked as she put the number next to her on the table.

Frankie raised his chin defiantly. "Would you have said yes?"

J.T. refused to lie. "No."

"That's why I didn't ask."

What was she going to *do* with the boy? "Don't you think I would have gotten a little suspicious when he came to the door again?"

His thin shoulders lifted and fell. The look in his eyes was distant. He pushed away his plate. "I didn't think you'd even be here. You hardly ever are, you know." A deaf person could have heard the accusation.

Familiar, worn territory. J.T. was too tired tonight to argue through it, knowing there was no winning. "I have a responsibility, Francis—"

"Yeah." Frankie rose, throwing down his napkin. "To everybody else." He stormed out of the room, almost running into Norma. Norma took a step back to avoid spilling coffee all over the floor.

With a look of disapproval Norma set down the empty cup and saucer, placing the coffeepot next to it in front of J.T. Norma looked at the boy's plate and shook her head as she picked it up. "It's his diet."

Preoccupied, the statement confused J.T. "What?"

"He doesn't eat enough greens. Makes him irritable. He should eat his greens."

"Another observation via the magic of public television programming?" J.T. asked wearily.

"You're never too old to learn." The implication was clear as Norma looked at J.T. "Finished?" J.T. nodded absently in reply. Norma picked up both plates, then crossed back to the kitchen. "I don't know why I bother cooking for you people. You never eat anything. The Brady Bunch never did that to Alice."

The kitchen door squeaked as it opened and then swung closed again.

"Alice had a cheerier disposition," J.T. said loudly. The only answer was the sounds of the kitchen TV. "No one listens to me, anyway."

J.T. sighed as she poured herself half a cup of coffee, then sat, looking into it. She wished she could see some answers there, wished that things were really as simple as Francis thought they were. Lately nothing was simple. There never seemed to be enough time to do anything right. Never enough time to enjoy anything.

Yet if she took a minute to breathe, she was afraid everything would crumble around her. And then where would the two of them be? Broke, that was where. It was all on her shoulders, and there were times that she was so weary of it, weary of fighting, weary of trying to keep body and soul together.

J.T. shook her head, pushing the thought away. What was wrong with her lately, anyway? She should be happy. She was young and reasonably successful. She had her own business, her own home. She glanced around the tastefully furnished dining room. Every last stitch was hers. She had bought this house after the divorce. Even now the word made her shiver. Nothing in the world had left her so cold, so hopeless. A frightened young woman of twenty-four with a little boy.

The money for the down payment had come from her parents. It was the last money she had ever accepted from them, no matter how tight things got afterward. There were months, she remembered, when Norma had worked without pay, refusing to leave, knowing how lost they'd be without her. J.T. realized she loved Norma the way she never had her own mother. Eventually J.T. had managed to pay her parents back with interest, buying back the first piece of her self-respect. It had been a long, hard road upward from that point.

She thought of her parents and realized there was still a pang there. She never could reach them. She probably never would. They had given her the money not because they loved her, but because she was their daughter and that was what was done. Proper behavior had always been so important to them. Love wasn't a subject that came up. Ever. She had been a model daughter because they had expected it. She had no idea if they loved her or her sister, Adriana. Or each other for that matter. She had grown up yearning for love, for someone to care. Her parents had been too removed and Adriana had been completely self-absorbed.

Damn, what brought this on?

It was that...that man! J.T. turned the brunt of her emotional turmoil on him, looking at the telephone number next to her elbow. Muttering a retort under her breath, J.T. forgot about her coffee and picked up the scrap of paper with his phone number written on it. She crossed to the telephone in the living room.

Placing the paper on the table next to the phone, she angrily jabbed out the numbers, then stopped. In her anger she had hit the wrong ones. Taking a breath to steady herself, she tried again, this time with success.

"Marino and McClellan."

The masculine voice surprised her. She had expected a secretary to answer. Glancing at her watch, she saw that it was almost seven o'clock. Her conversation with Frankie had gotten her so upset that she hadn't realized it was late.

Logically no one should have been in the office. Maybe she had gotten the night watchman.

"Hello?" the deep voice asked.

"Um, sorry. I was calling Mr. McClellan—" Her stomach was churning nervously. She hadn't felt this way since she had waited for Jarrod Anderson to ask her to the senior prom—and he hadn't. This was totally out of character for her now.

"This is McClellan." He recognized her voice the moment she spoke. It had echoed in his brain for two days now. "What can I do for you, J.T.?"

Caught completely off guard, J.T.'s mind went blank. She took a deep breath, upbraiding herself. If her clients saw her now, they'd have second thoughts about hiring her firm to do their accounts, she thought disparagingly. "Um, you're working rather late, Sh-Shad." Wonderful, just wonderful.

"Is this a survey?" Shad asked, amused.

Was he laughing at her? "Mr. McClellan—"

"Yes, Ms. Mayne?"

He *was* laughing at her. J.T. became the woman her clients relied on to hold their hand through IRS audits and fight for their entries. "I'm calling about tomorrow."

"Tomorrow?"

"Don't act innocent with me, Mr. McClellan." She saw Norma looking in from the kitchen and she turned her back, lowering her voice.

"I wouldn't dream of it. I'm not that good an actor."

Now he was bragging about his so-called sexual prowess. Typical male. She had him pegged right from the start. "You have no right inviting yourself over."

"Actually, he invited me."

"Don't try to play with semantics, McClellan, you—"

Her angry tone ceased to annoy him. He could picture her, warm and vibrant, her passions raised for different reasons. "What would you like me to play?"

J.T.'s eyes narrowed. "Look—"

He was through playing with words. It was time she got a few things straight. "No, I think you should look. It might save you some embarrassment. Ladies as pretty as you shouldn't have to eat crow. Frankie called me yesterday and asked if I would help him with his science project. It just so happens, if I catch up on everything by tonight, that I'm free tomorrow. I told him I'd come if he cleared it with you. He promised he would. Apparently he's having some trouble with that stage."

J.T. realized she was twisting the phone cord and now had her finger stuck. But what he said caught her attention. "You're working late because of Francis?"

"Yes." He heard the astonishment in her voice. "Why is that so surprising?"

She managed to pull her finger free. "Why are you doing this?" The boy meant nothing to him.

"I told you. He asked me."

There had to be more to it than that. The man was too good to be true. And nothing, she had learned, was too good to be true. Nothing. Just who and what *was* this man? She slid onto the couch, pulling the phone with her. Her resolve never to let him set foot in her house was beginning to waver. "You never did answer my question."

Shad smiled. It was going to be all right, he thought. "Which question was that?"

"The one I asked you on the way to the ball game— about who you are." She cleared her throat. Her voice was cracking.

"Okay. Full name, Shadrach Michael McClellan. Age, thirty-two. Height, six feet on a good day. Weight, 163 pounds if I stay away from Sunday dinners at Ma's. Occupation, I'm a contractor. Status, single, currently unattached." He waited.

The queasy feeling was returning and she told herself that it was because of dinner, or lack thereof. Finding out that the man was single had nothing to do with it. "I didn't need to know the last part."

"Maybe, but I do. Are you?"

She shifted in her seat. "Am I what?"

"Attached?"

Her expression hardened as she thought of Pete. "No, and I don't intend to be." She swallowed and kept herself from playing with the cord again. With a deliberate movement she placed her free hand on the sofa and kept it there.

He picked up on her tone. She was divorced. "Hurt you that badly, did he?"

She wasn't going to give in to the sympathy in his voice. She wasn't going to allow herself to lean, to accept comfort, no matter how much she wanted to. She was supposed to be past that point, way past. "I don't think that's any of your business, Mr. McClellan."

"No, you're right." Yet, he added silently.

His agreeableness took her aback. What was there about this man that halted her in her tracks every time she got up a full head of steam?

"I suppose it wouldn't hurt for you to come over and help Francis with his project. I'm not very good when it comes to science," she admitted.

"Different people are good at different things. I'm sure you have a lot of other terrific qualities."

He had to stop this. "Are you deliberately trying to be likable?"

"Trying my darnedest. How am I doing?"

"Got yourself invited over, didn't you?"

"Yes."

She heard the grin in his voice. "Don't push it."

"Why do I get the feeling that when you're talking to me, you're actually shadowboxing with someone else?"

He was getting too close to the truth for her. "You are very likable."

"Thank you. You didn't mean that as a compliment, did you?" he asked knowingly.

J.T. closed her eyes. It had been a long, hard day and it was getting harder by the moment. "I don't want to like you." *I don't want to leave myself open to things that happened before.*

"Why not?"

"Because I just don't," she insisted.

"Would it upset you if I told you that I don't share your goal?"

Her hands were clenched. He was tying her up in knots. She shouldn't let him do that. Where was all this newfound strength she thought she had? "I don't care about your goals, McClellan. I do care about my son. If you want to help him with his project, you're welcome to come over, if not, don't. Is that clear?"

"Yes, ma'am," he said with a docility she distrusted. "Answer me one thing."

She sighed, exasperated. It always seemed to come to that with him. "What?"

"What's the J.T. stand for?"

It was a harmless enough question, she supposed. "Julienne Trent. Trent was my maiden name."

"Julienne." When he rolled it over his tongue, she felt a shiver travel through her, mimicking the jolt she had felt when he'd touched her. "Nice name."

"Takes too long to say," she said briskly. "I use J.T. for business purposes."

"I've got time."

She felt his smile, warm and sexy. She knew trouble when she heard it. "I don't. Goodbye, McClellan."

"Good night, Julienne."

J.T. hung up with a slam, then stared at the phone accusingly. She'd known it was a mistake to tell him her name as soon as she had said it. For two cents she'd call him back and tell him not to come.

The receiver stayed in the cradle.

J.T.'s doubts about the wisdom of allowing Shad to come over grew and finally exploded when she opened the door, balancing files and a briefcase, the next morning at nine. He was dressed casually in a bright blue T-shirt that absolutely gripped his biceps. It was tucked into a pair of faded jeans that looked as if they had been molded to him since birth.

His eyes met hers and told her he knew exactly what she had on her mind. J.T. could have punched him. "Hi. Frankie around?"

"That's the term for it." She held the door open wider. "He's been around, bouncing off walls since six this morning." It was all she had time to say before Francis sailed down the stairs and came to a skidding halt by the front door.

"Hi, Shad." Frankie grabbed his arm, already tugging him toward the family room. "Ready?"

"As I'll ever be." He laughed affectionately at his eagerness. Frankie reminded him of himself as a boy after Salvator had come into his life. Everything seemed brighter, better with Angelo's father there. In a way, he mused, he was repaying a debt, passing the seeds of hope along. "This, I believe, is for you." He presented him with the autographed baseball, and Frankie squealed with joy.

It was then that J.T. noticed he had brought a duffel bag with him and it was obviously full. He picked it up by the tie strings and brought it into the house as he crossed the threshold.

"Are you planning on moving in?" she asked warily.

"Is that an invitation?"

"No!" She bit the word off quickly, and he gave her a knowing look that made her twice as uncomfortable. "I just meant..." Her voice trailed off as she pointed at the bag.

Shad looked down. "No, this just has some of the things I thought we might need for the project." He looked her over. She was wearing another one of her suits and was obviously on her way out. "I take it you won't be joining us?"

She didn't have time for this. The Whitney accounts were due Monday, and she didn't feel confident enough about Gary's ability to do a good job. She was all set to leave for the office and prepare notes.

And yet something wouldn't let her go.

She paused at the front door, undecided, leaning her files on the hall table. "No, I—" she began.

Shad put down the duffel bag and reached for the files. "Here, those must be heavy. Want me to take them to the car?" He was aware of Frankie shifting impatiently from foot to foot. He didn't want to make him feel as if he had been shunted to the background again, but he thought that getting J.T. to stay was important. For both of them.

J.T. bit her lower lip. She could work here in her den as well as down at the office. After all, she had almost all the files she needed.

"No." She made her decision, surprising both her son and herself. But not Shad. "To the den. I'm staying."

Frankie stared at her. There was a hint of a confused smile on his lips.

Shad merely nodded. "That's good."

J.T. found she had no answer for that, so she led the way to her den at the other end of the house.

"Just put them on the desk." She pointed at it needlessly.

She turned and caught the smile on his face. Once again she was struck by the absolute sexiness of it. It was a smile that curled her toes and made her itch. There was attraction in the air between them. Pure physical attraction. It was that simple. And yet not simple at all. Not for her.

His smile was disarming.

That was what he kept doing to her at every turn. Defusing her. Dismantling her. Making her fall apart bit by bit. Away from this man, she was an efficient, competent businesswoman. But there was something about him that undid all that. He took away her poise, her carefully built-up self-confidence, making it fall away as if it was a sham. As if he secretly knew that beneath it all, she was still that young, frightened woman who had suddenly found herself deserted, with a small child to care for and no one to buffer her from the outside world. No one to love her and tell her that everything was going to be all right.

"Do you want it over here?" He placed her briefcase and the files in the center of the desk. He noticed that it was all very neat and precise. Orderly, like her.

"It's fine." Her throat felt oddly tight as the words forced themselves out.

"All right, then I guess I'd better roll up my sleeves and get to it, then."

"They already are rolled up," she murmured, her eyes skimming the hard muscles. She was unaffected, she told herself. Totally, utterly unaffected. "I mean, they're short.

The sleeves." It was just getting worse and worse with each word. Any moment now and she'd be stuttering like an idiot.

His nearness didn't help the situation any. She felt heat rush between their bodies. Heat, for heaven's sake. It was because of the size of the room. Why was it that she had never noticed how small this room was before? And why did she always seem to be running out of breath around him?

Shad looked needlessly down at his arms. "You noticed."

He knew how disoriented he was getting her, damn him. This was amusing him. She wanted him out of here.

And yet she didn't.

She was turning into a masochist, she thought. "How's your sister?" she heard herself asking, knowing it was a ploy to make him stay just a moment longer. Why couldn't she make up her mind?

He rested his hand on the doorknob. Why did everything he do seem so rakish? And attractive.

"Restless. But then Dottie's always been like that. She likes to run headlong into things. The cast makes that a little difficult."

"Then she's home?"

"Not exactly. She's staying with me until the cast comes off. She and her menagerie."

"Menagerie?"

"She's a sucker for pets. They have to stay somewhere while she recovers."

"So you're putting them all up?"

He nodded.

He had taken his sister and assorted pets in. There was a lot to be said for a man who cared that much about his sister. Or for a man who took the time to help a teenage boy he wasn't even related to.

A lot to be said, but she wasn't going to say it. Not if her life depended on it. Which, in a rather perverse way, it did.

Shad slowly closed the door behind him as he left. She had absolutely no idea why that felt so intimate. But it did.

It made her realize even more that somehow, though she might present a cool, sophisticated face to the world, Shad McClellan knew her secret. That she wasn't what she seemed. That the very competent Ms. J. T. Mayne wanted more than anything else to succeed only in one area, the area where she had failed so miserably. The area of love. First her husband had left her, now her son was drifting away, and she hadn't a clue how to stop it or change it.

J.T. sank down into her chair, the tips of her fingers pyramiding before her. She stared at the closed door. How did he know? And why did it matter to her that he did?

With a shake of her head J.T. turned her attention to the files. Numbers she could always handle. It was life that confused her.

Life, and a man called Shad McClellan.

Chapter Six

She had no idea so much time had passed. The hands of the antique clock on her desk indicated that it was just after eleven-thirty. She had been locked in this little room with her files and her calculator for over two hours.

Making note of the last figure she had calculated on the ledger, J.T. paused, took off her glasses and rubbed the bridge of her nose. A mild headache was building behind her right temple. Maybe it was time to take a break. She doubted that Francis was still working on his project, but if he was, maybe she could offer him a little help. Mr. Science Project had probably left over an hour ago.

Funny, she hadn't heard his car pull away.

J.T. stretched. The muscles in her neck and shoulders were aching the way they always did when she worked long hours.

Could he possibly still be here?

Curious, she got up from her desk and crossed to the door. Cracking it open, she heard the sound of Francis's voice coming from the family room. Francis had probably invited one of his friends over. It seemed impossible that a good-looking, unattached man would give up his entire Saturday to help a young boy he had no ties to. Still, J.T. smoothed down her hair before she went to the family room to see for herself.

He was here.

Her stomach tightened just a little before she consciously forced herself to relax. "Well," she said a tad too brightly, "how did the project go?" She crossed to the sofa, telling herself that there was absolutely no reason why she should feel awkward in her own family room. But she did.

Shad was sitting crossed-legged on the floor across from Francis. A littered coffee table was between them.

"It's still going," Shad told her, looking up. There were chunks of colored clay, wire cutters, broken pieces of what looked as if they had once been coat hangers and colored paper all arranged on a huge sheet of brown wrapping paper. Several astronomy books encircled the mess, open to various pages depicting the different planets.

J.T. picked up the book closest to her and thumbed through it. "Where did you get all this?" she asked Francis.

"Shad brought it." Frankie all but beamed proudly. "It's for my project."

She met Shad's eyes over the top of the book, but still addressed her question to Francis. "How did he know what to bring?"

"I told him." Frankie looked worshipfully at Shad. "He listens." The inference was clear.

Time to defuse the conversation before there was another confrontation between the two factions, Shad thought. "I also had a pad and pencil available," Shad said quickly. "Otherwise I can't remember a darn thing. It's a habit I developed a long time ago." He pulled out a small pad from his back pocket. It was slightly bent from adhering to his body.

Without thinking J.T. reached out and touched the offered pad. It was still warm. She dropped her hand self-consciously. Shad looked amused as he slipped the pad back into his pocket.

"Well, I'd better leave you two to your work, then." Feeling the need to retreat, she turned on her heel. Shad was quick to spring to his feet, catching her hand. J.T. stared at him, surprised. This was getting to be a habit, being caught off guard by him. It wasn't a habit she wanted to cultivate.

"No, stay. We'd like some impartial input." He gestured toward the unfinished model on the table with his free hand. "What do you think?"

J.T. looked at the model for the first time. She circled it slowly. "Looks interesting," she ventured tentatively.

"Sounds like the kiss of death to me." Frankie groaned dejectedly.

"Do you know what it is?" he asked J.T.

He was putting her on the spot again, she thought, annoyed. She looked back at one of the books on the floor. "The solar system." It was a lucky guess. It didn't look like much of anything yet.

"See," he said to Frankie. "It's coming along." He believed in picking up the bright side of everything. "We just have to keep at it." Frankie groaned louder and covered his face. "Hey." He took hold of Frankie's shoulders, and the boy looked up, resigned. "Nothing good was ever easy."

He was looking at her son, but for some odd reason J.T. felt as if he was talking to her.

"Good things take time and work. And we've got all afternoon." He looked toward J.T. "If that's all right with your mom."

This time it was a little easier to agree. "It's all right with me."

How did he do it? she wondered. How did he make communicating with Francis seem so easy, so effortless? He had known him for less than a week and he was getting along with her son far better than she had of late.

Francis's face burst into a smile. Putting up with Shad was worth this, J.T. thought. Maybe in time she and Francis would get back on this footing again. She could only hope. And maybe take a few notes.

"Care to join in?" J.T. had turned to leave, but his question stopped her. The invitation, softly voiced, had almost a seductive quality to it.

Yes, was the instant reply that came to her lips, but she buried it.

Instead, J.T. glanced over her shoulder toward the den. There was still some work left to be done on the account she had brought home. Some of the figures still didn't tally, and she hated to let it go. Her resolution to always finish a job she started warred with her instincts as a mother. She looked toward Shad, and the half smile on his face tipped the scales. The account would still be there in an hour or so.

She raised her eyebrows in a gesture of helplessness. "What do you want me to do?" She looked at the collection of things on the table and felt instantly inept. She had never been particularly good with her hands.

Just stand there, looking the way you do, and that'll be enough for me, Shad thought. He grabbed a hunk of clay and handed it to her. "You can start by rolling this into a ball."

She felt his fingertips lightly cross her palm and tried not to show that it affected her. J.T. examined the clay with undue care. "Any particular reason?"

"Well, planets are usually round."

"I know that." She tossed her head and several pins slipped. Automatically she reached to secure them.

"Don't," Shad urged. "Let me see what it looks like down."

"I—" Nothing else followed the initial protest. It was as if the words were trapped in her throat.

"It's pretty," Frankie told him.

"I had a hunch."

Just to please Francis, she thought, surprised at her son's compliment. "All right," J.T. answered slowly, pulling the rest of the pins free. Thick chestnut hair tumbled down in waves past her shoulders.

The look Shad gave her warmed her blood. Magic, J.T. thought. He could weave magic. This man, she thought, was dangerous. Dangerous because he was so easy to like, so easy to—

She caught her breath. "What planet am I making?"

"What do you say, Frank? Shall we let her make Pluto?"

"Okay." It was easy to see that Francis would have agreed to absolutely any suggestion Shad made.

"Pluto it is," J.T. said, sitting down on the floor next to her son.

Shad laughed and the low, masculine sound vibrated through her, setting off that odd tingle again. It buzzed and hummed through the core of her body, making it vibrate. Making her ache for things she hadn't felt in a very long time.

"We're going where no man has gone before—" Shad told her with a wink.

"No *one* has gone before," Norma corrected, carrying a basket of laundry through the room on her way up the stairs.

"Sorry, I stand corrected." Shad nodded in the housekeeper's direction. "Need help with that?" he asked before she made it to the stairs.

"I'm fine. You just keep on doing what you're doing," Norma called back as she trudged up the stairs.

Shad turned and looked directly into J.T.'s eyes before he reached for another length of wire. "I intend to," he said softly.

Nerves awoke and stood on end for no other reason than because he looked at her that way. "Um, is this all right for a science project?" J.T. nodded toward the model.

"Sure, why?" Wariness had slipped back into Frankie's voice as he answered.

J.T. shrugged. Wrong thing to say. Again. "No reason, but I thought you were supposed to prove something."

"That's for the scientifically-minded," Shad told her. "The dreamers—" he slid a finger down Frankie's upturned nose "—dream. They see things scientists don't."

"That's very poetic," J.T. observed wryly.

"I suppose it is." He snapped off the second end of the wire.

He wasn't going to get away with it that easily. "It's also a way of getting out of doing an experiment."

He laughed. "That, too. But Frankie cleared it with his teacher. And this way I can use a little of my expertise to help. Okay—" he pointed at the clay in J.T.'s hand "—start molding."

They worked for the better part of the afternoon. Shad guided Francis into doing most of the project himself, though he wasn't slow in offering suggestions. Mostly, J.T.

noted, he was lavish with praise, even though there were one or two moments when Francis looked ready to give up, especially when the solar system refused to stay mounted the first time. The main vertical wire snapped under the increasing weight of the planets they were adding.

"Oh, it's no use," Frankie muttered.

"Frankie," Shad said, and it was the first time J.T. had heard him use a stern tone of voice, "there is *always* use in trying. I don't want to hear about you ever giving up. If you give up on the small stuff, how are you ever going to bear up to the bigger things in life?"

Francis shrugged without answering. J.T. saw that his eyes were slightly misted in frustrated embarrassment. She wanted to tell her son that it didn't matter, but she knew her words would be rejected. Though it was hard, J.T. held her tongue.

Calmly Shad began shaping another, thicker length of wire. "Fact is, you won't," he said, answering his own question. "You'll snap just like that wire did. The trick in life is making sure you're too thick to snap. That's how you fool life—and get the most out of it." He handed Frankie the wire, then tugged on his hair affectionately. "Got it, kid?"

Frankie nodded, grinning this time. "Got it." He took the wire from Shad and began painstakingly to attach the solar system again.

"Quite a speech," J.T. commented, grudgingly admiring the gradual metamorphosis she was seeing in her son. Nothing she said could have evoked it. Shad had a way about him; she'd give him that.

Shad leaned, resting his back against the sofa. "I don't make speeches, Julienne. I say things I believe in. There's a difference."

"Oh?"

"Speeches are to motivate people to get behind you in something. I just want Frankie to learn how to roll with the punches. It's the best thing anyone can ever teach you in life." It's something, he thought, looking at the shadow of pain in J.T.'s eyes, that someone should have taught her somewhere along the line.

J.T. felt he was seeing through her again. Purposely she averted her eyes and watched Francis's progress. "I certainly seemed to have gotten a bargain when I asked your sister to come by."

"Lady," he said, grinning, "you don't know the half of it."

It sounded like a promise.

"How's this?" Frankie asked proudly.

He turned to look at the effort. "Good. But Saturn's rings are slipping. Here." Shad rose to his knees. "Maybe if we do this." He tried various positions, then secured the rings with a simple pushpin. "There, that'll do it. I think we've got the start of a pretty good solar system on our hands. What do you think?"

"I think it's terrific." Frankie's eyes shone. "Thank you."

He patted the boy's arm. "The pleasure's all mine, Frankie."

"How did you learn to be so handy?" J.T. brushed the clay from her hands. She moved to rise. Shad took her hand in his and helped her up. She found herself standing far closer to him than she had intended. And liking it.

"Natural ability, I suppose."

"Oh, that's right. You're in construction." The words were stilted, forced, but she had to say something. She couldn't just stand there. "Doing it long?"

He wanted to kiss her. She looked so out of place, so lost. He wanted to show her that she wasn't. But there was

Frankie to think of. So he bided his time. "Since I was eleven."

That was awfully young, she thought. "Family business?"

"You might say that." Now she looked confused, adorably confused. He wasn't sure which expression he liked more. Probably one he hadn't seen yet, he mused. He wondered what desire would look like, flaming in her eyes. Just the prospect excited him. "My foster father owned the company."

"Foster father? You were an orphan?" She had always pictured orphans as sad, lonely people. There was nothing sad or lonely about Shad.

He watched as Frankie voluntarily began to clear bits of clay from the table. "Technically."

The scene left J.T. in awe. She couldn't remember when she had seen Francis clean up after himself without being prodded and threatened first, even in the best of times. She couldn't deny that Shad was having a good effect on the boy. Just a bad one on her. "I didn't know you could be one of those technically."

He laughed at the serious way she said it. "I always had Dottie, so I never really felt 'orphaned.' And when I was eleven, Salvator Marino took both of us in and we were part of a family again."

"You sound as if you're very close to your sister."

"I am." He heard the wistful way she said it. "Are you an only child?"

"No, but I might as well have been. My sister and I aren't very close at all. Mostly she just criticizes."

If Dottie hadn't been there in his life, things might have been different for him. A lot different. He empathized. "I'm sorry."

J.T. said nothing. She didn't know what had come over her, admitting that. She was a very private person. Her hurts were her own. He had a way of coaxing things out of her. It made her uncomfortable, and yet it was almost a relief to share things with someone. He kept confusing her, creating ambivalent feelings.

He saw the look that came over her face. It was as if a curtain had suddenly fallen down. "Did I say something wrong?"

J.T. shook her head. Before he could press her for an answer, Norma appeared with a tray of soft drinks.

"I'll be going out now," she informed J.T., setting the tray on the coffee table. She smiled approvingly at Shad, and J.T. could see that Norma was charmed right down to the crepe soles of her sneakers. "I'd stay, but I did promise my sister I'd go with her to catch that new movie." She looked at her watch, obviously debating the situation. "Of course, she's a grown woman and could go alone...."

The man was throwing everything off kilter, J.T. thought in amazement. He had gotten Francis to do schoolwork on a Saturday, her to forsake her work, and when had she *ever* heard Norma volunteer to miss a first-run movie? Or any movie for that matter?

"No, this is your afternoon off." J.T. ushered the shorter woman toward the door. "You go ahead and enjoy your movie. Tell us about it when you get back."

Norma peered into the room before she finally disappeared reluctantly through the door. "All right, if you insist." Then, as an afterthought, she raised herself on her toes and whispered, "If you let this one go, you're a lost cause."

J.T. shut the door. The last thing she needed was her housekeeper giving out advice to the lovelorn. She turned to see Shad regarding her thoughtfully, a smile on his face.

No, the last thing she needed was a man in her house who made her forget all her priorities and promises to herself. Man trouble, that was what she had. But she wasn't going to succumb. No dreams, no disappointments—that had been her rule to live by.

He was making her forget.

"What'll we do about dinner?" Frankie asked suddenly. "Pizza?" He looked toward Shad hopefully.

Shad seemed about to spring for a delivery when J.T. announced, "No, I'll cook."

Frankie stared at her. "You can cook?" Norma had always been the one who cooked. Either that, or they had take-out food.

"Yes, Frankie, I can cook." J.T. saw Francis exchange a pleased grin with Shad, and suddenly realized she had used her son's nickname without being aware of it. It had just slipped out. This man was affecting more things than she had thought. "I'll leave you two to your solar system and see what there is in the refrigerator to work with."

"So tell me," Shad began after finishing a meal that in his estimation could only be equaled by his foster mother's skills, "how is it that a lady who looks the way you do and cooks the way you do isn't married?"

She watched Frankie run off to the family room after saying he wanted to try "just one more thing" on their model. Self-consciously, J.T. rose, taking her plate to the sink. "I believe the standard answer here is 'just lucky, I guess.'" She turned to pick up the other plates, only to have Shad hand them to her.

"There's nothing lucky about doing without love. You know, Julienne," he said casually, "you can't keep running from relationships forever." Deftly he cleared the table, bringing the other dishes to the counter next to the sink.

"I can if I want to." Her voice was tight.

"Maybe I won't let you." There was a soft, promissory note in his voice.

She ran water into the sink, watching the bubbles build. Just like the emotions going on inside of her. "I wish you wouldn't call me that."

"Why?" He reached past her and sank a glass into the water. It bobbed back up stubbornly. "It's your name, isn't it? Why do you use initials?"

She wished he wouldn't pry. Initials took away her sexuality. They took away the fear of being compromised because she was a woman. "I told you, it's faster." And safer.

"Some things are nicer slow." He picked up the large serving platter. One piece of chicken Diana was left.

Suddenly J.T. had an image of making love with him. Slowly. She dropped the clean glass back into the water and mumbled an oath. She had to keep a tighter rein on her mind.

"Put that over there, please." She indicated the platter and nodded toward the far counter, next to the refrigerator. Her voice was shaky.

"Sure thing. Where do you keep the foil?"

"In the pantry." She heard him open the door. Odd how they just fell into working together like this, she thought, then stopped herself short. There was no reason to let her mind wander like this. Nothing would come of it.

He found room for the platter in the refrigerator, then turned back to J.T. "Well, the chicken's all tucked away for the night," he told her. "Why don't you let me help you with the dishes?"

"You don't have to." He kept making her feel awkward.

"No, but I'd still like to." He picked up a towel and began drying the dishes she was lining up on the rack in the other sink.

To hide her nervousness J.T. concentrated on the dishes. "Thank you," she mumbled.

He grinned to himself. "You're welcome." A handful of silverware found its way into the drawer, one by one after he toweled them dry. Each rattled against the one before. It was the only sound besides the running water. "So, what were you doing in the den?"

She felt safe talking about work. "Accounting. I'm an accountant."

"Boss a slave driver?"

She looked up, wondering if he was baiting her. "I *am* the boss."

"Even worse," he said knowingly.

She turned to look at him, a dish suspended in her hand. "What?"

He took the dish from her. "People who work for themselves tend to be even harder to please than other people." Putting the plate down, he took another from the rack. "When did you get started?"

"After Pete left." She stopped. She hadn't meant that to come out. She should have realized there was no such thing as a safe topic when she was talking to him.

Shad put the stacked dishes away. She couldn't help noticing how effortless this all was to him. Was there anything that didn't come naturally to him? "Did you have a degree then?"

"No. I went to school at night." She thought of the long hours spent studying, the even longer hours spent working to keep body and soul together at the two jobs she juggled in order to pay the bills. But it had all been worth it.

He thought of her alone with Frankie. "Pretty brave of you."

She shrugged, telling herself that his praise didn't matter. "I had no choice. I would have liked to have withdrawn from the world, maybe gone catatonic for a while. But I had a son to raise. I didn't have the luxury of nursing hurt feelings. I had to get on with my life for his sake."

He thought of the call she had made to Dottie. "Hasn't he gotten lost in the shuffle? Seems to me you're rather successful."

The last pot done, she pulled the plug out of the drain, watching the water swirl out. "I am." She didn't want to launch into the problems the firm was having hanging on to its accounts. It wasn't any of his business.

"So—" he leaned his hip against the sink, folding his towel "—how about kicking back a little?"

Didn't he understand? "If I do, everything will start sliding back. We'll lose clients."

"We," he echoed. "Then you don't run the whole show."

"No, I have three accountants." Why was she bothering to explain all this to him? He didn't belong in her life. He had no right to ask all these questions.

"They're all incompetent I take it."

She bristled, taking offense for them. "Of course not."

"Then what are you worried about? Afraid to find out you're not indispensable?" He saw her open her mouth to respond, but he wouldn't let her get in a word. "Because you're not, you know. Not to a company, not to a client. But to him—" he jerked a thumb in the direction of the family room "—well, that's a different story. Right now you *are* indispensable." He leaned closer. Too close for either one of them to deal with objectively. "I'd hold on to that if I were you."

She would have taken a step back if the sink hadn't stopped her progress. So she held her ground, her knees weak, her resolve struggling to stay strong. "You seem to have some inside track on that knowledge." Angrily she took the towel from him. Who did he think he was, coming into her life and telling her what to do? "Just how many kids do you have?"

"None," he answered casually, taking another step closer. "But I was one once." His eyes held hers. "And I remember what it was like to want someone who wasn't there."

J.T. looked down at the floor. She really didn't want to know this. Knowing would weaken her resolve. He would become more of a person, a friend, a—

If she held him at bay, if she didn't know anything about him, he would remain a stranger. That was easier to handle. She couldn't deal with the alternative. "I'm sorry. I didn't mean to—"

"No, you're much too proper to 'mean to.'" He threaded his fingers softly through her hair, framing her face.

J.T.'s breath caught in her throat as she pulled the dish towel taut between her hands, creating a frail barrier between them. She had nothing else. Her voice failed her.

He thought of a frightened doe frozen in the headlights of a car. Why was she afraid of something so natural, so right?

Slowly, so slowly that it felt as if time had stood still, he lowered his mouth to hers. And then his lips touched hers so softly that she ached inside. That was it, just the barest touch. Nothing more. And yet it was so much more. He couldn't even begin to guess how much, she thought.

"What was that for?" The question came out in a whisper. Her throat seemed to have swollen shut.

He ran his fingers through her hair, smiling. It felt soft and silky, just as he had known it would. He smiled into her eyes. "Openers."

Frankie's excited voice shattered the moment as he called from the family room for Shad to "Come see."

He sighed patiently. "I'd better go see what he wants."

J.T. could only mutely nod, then sag a little as he left the room.

Chapter Seven

Openers?

J.T. stood staring at Shad's departing figure. Openers? Just what was it he thought was being opened here? She didn't want anything to be opened. She *liked* things just the way they were, tightly sealed, controlled. She had her son and business and that was all she needed. *All*. She didn't need a man who was just passing through her life to "open" anything.

Her breath slightly ragged, she leaned against the counter and dragged a hand through her hair. She blinked several times in succession, as if trying to focus her mind again.

His kiss, which lit up portions of her being that had been pushed into the dark for so long, told her she was lying to herself, that there was an additional, neglected need.

Well, it was going to remain neglected. Living the life she led was less chaotic and infinitely more reassuring, at least emotionally. She wasn't about to plunge into an abyss again. She wasn't about to put her heart on the line an-

NO RISK, NO OBLIGATION TO BUY... NOW OR EVER!

GUARANTEED

PLAY "ROLL A DOUBLE" AND GET AS MANY AS SIX GIFTS!

HERE'S HOW TO PLAY:

1. Peel off label from front cover. Place it in space provided at right. With a coin, carefully scratch off the silver dice. This makes you eligible to receive one or more free books, and possibly other gifts, depending on what is revealed beneath the scratch-off area.

2. You'll receive brand-new Silhouette Romance™ novels. When you return this card, we'll rush you the books and gifts you qualify for ABSOLUTELY FREE!

3. Then, if we don't hear from you, every month we'll send you 6 additional novels to read and enjoy. You can return them and owe nothing, but if you decide to keep them, you'll pay only $2.25 per book—a savings of 25¢ each off the cover price.

4. When you subscribe to the Silhouette Reader Service™, you'll also get our newsletter, as well as additional free gifts from time to time.

5. You must be completely satisfied. You may cancel at any time simply by sending us a note or a shipping statement marked "cancel" or by returning any shipment to us at our expense.

You'll look like a million dollars when you wear this elegant necklace! It's a generous 20 inches long and each link is double-soldered for strength and durability.

"ROLL A DOUBLE!"

PLACE LABEL HERE

SCRATCH HERE

?

SEE CLAIM CHART BELOW

215 CIS ACLU
(U-SIL-R-09/91)

YES! I have placed my label from the front cover into the space provided above and scratched off the silver dice. Please rush me the free book(s) and gift(s) that I am entitled to. I understand that I am under no obligation to purchase any books, as explained on the opposite page.

NAME

ADDRESS   APT.

CITY   STATE   ZIP CODE

CLAIM CHART

🎲🎲	**4 FREE BOOKS PLUS FREE 20" NECKLACE PLUS MYSTERY BONUS GIFT**
🎲🎲	**3 FREE BOOKS PLUS BONUS GIFT**
🎲🎲	**2 FREE BOOKS**

CLAIM NO.37-829

SILHOUETTE ''NO RISK'' GUARANTEE

DETACH AND MAIL CARD TODAY!

BUSINESS REPLY MAIL

FIRST CLASS MAIL   PERMIT NO. 717   BUFFALO, NY

POSTAGE WILL BE PAID BY ADDRESSEE

SILHOUETTE READER SERVICE
3010 WALDEN AVE
PO BOX 1867
BUFFALO NY 14240-9952

NO POSTAGE
NECESSARY
IF MAILED
IN THE
UNITED STATES

other time. Just who the hell did this man think he was, spending the better part of the day molding clay and cutting wires with her son, then weakening her resolve and taking advantage?

She wasn't going to take this lying down!

But you'd like to, a small, wistful voice whispered in the dark recesses of her mind. She ran her fingers across her lips, a small smile playing with the corners of her mouth. She sighed. In order to be victorious one had to really want to win.

She told herself that she did.

Frustrated, J.T. scooped up the dish towel that had fallen on the floor and threw it in the general direction of the sink. Then, using her indignation as a shield, she marched into the family room.

"McClellan—" she began, ready to evict him from her house, science project or no science project.

"Yes?" Shad looked up from the coffee table. He was back on the rug again, supervising. "Frankie wanted to add moons." He gestured at the model. Delicately fashioned spheres cut out of foil hung suspended from the main supporting frame. It was really beginning to look like the hand of a professional had worked on it. Or guided its creation. She couldn't have done that for Frankie. And she still didn't understand why he had. "Well, what do you think?"

"I think...I think—" J.T. got no farther. She wanted to give him a piece of her mind for having taken advantage like that in the kitchen, for thinking what he was undoubtedly thinking. But seeing the model and Frankie's obvious pride in it took away some of her fire.

Blowing a gust of air out slowly, her eyes warning him that they *weren't* finished yet, J.T. murmured, "It looks very—"

"Professional?" Frankie supplied hopefully. Clearly this was his baby, and he was very protective of it. The young boy laced his fingers together and almost looked shy. Shy? Her son? "Shad said it looked very professional."

J.T. pressed her lips together, then nodded. "Yes, it does look very professional." Giving in to an impulse, she ruffled Frankie's hair. Frankie looked up, then grinned broadly, looking every inch the sunny twelve-year-old.

Her heart full, J.T. forgave Shad everything. Temporarily.

"I think it's going to be a real hit," Frankie declared, scrambling to his feet. Then he looked shy again. "The science fair's next Friday afternoon at the school gym. Can you come?" The question was directed toward Shad.

Shad passed his hand over the back of his neck, thinking of his schedule. The bid for the mall was next Friday morning. That was in Malibu. It would be tight. "What time?"

His eyes were hopeful. It almost broke J.T.'s heart as she remembered herself in the exact same situation. Then it had been a play and she had asked her father to attend. He never did.

"Three o'clock."

He ran his finger down Frankie's nose playfully. "I'll give it my best shot," he promised.

It was good enough for Frankie.

Shad saw the look on J.T.'s face. She didn't trust him. Somehow he was going to get her to open up, to tell him what lurked in the dark corners of her life that made her so skittish. The simple kiss he had sampled had assured him that his suspicions were right on the money. There was passion there, existing just below the surface. He was determined to bring it out. And soon.

"You'll be there, too," he said to J.T. It was a statement rather than a question, as if he was feeding her lines to say.

Frankie turned, waiting for his mother's answer.

It would take some effort, but whatever it took she would manage it. She wanted Frankie to know that no matter how things might seem at times, he was first in her life. "I'll be there, too," J.T. assured Shad, then turned to see the pleased grin on Frankie's face before he hid it, striving to be nonchalant about his mother's promise.

Frankie might have been nonchalant, but Shad's approval was evident in the way he smiled at J.T. It went right through her, rekindling the feelings his kiss had generated just moments before. She resisted its effects even as she reveled in them.

"Well," Frankie rose reluctantly, "I've still got that book report due on Monday morning."

"Need any help?" Shad got up, carefully depositing bits of foil onto the table.

Frankie shook his head sheepishly. "First, I've got to read the book."

"That's a good start," Shad agreed. A quick look in J.T.'s direction forestalled her impulse to lecture about leaving things to the last minute.

Frankie nodded. "Night. And thanks," he tossed over his shoulder as he retreated. The words were meant for Shad.

"I was going to reprimand him," J.T. said, breaking the momentary silence that made her horribly uncomfortable. She felt as if she needed to be talking, moving, filling the space between them somehow. She felt like a gangly girl again, standing in front of her speech class and at a loss as to what to do with her hands. Mechanically she began gathering the remnants of the project.

"I know."

She glanced up, puzzled. "How did you know?"

Shad sat on the edge of the sofa, watching her. She seemed edgy again. "You had that look in your eye."

A bit of clay got under her nail and she frowned at it, and Shad. "You don't know me well enough to recognize a 'look' in my eye."

He leaned forward, his knee brushing against her shoulder. He felt her quiver slightly. "Don't I?"

J.T. dusted off her hands, giving up the pretense of tidying. "Look, McClellan, I appreciate what you've done for my son, but—"

He cocked his head, an insolent grin creasing his lips. Insolent and, oh, so appealing. She held fast to her resolve. He wasn't going to get to her. He wasn't.

"I scare the hell out of you?"

"That *wasn't* what I was about to say," she insisted stubbornly.

"No, but that's what you were thinking." He shifted closer, taking her hands in his. It seemed to cut off her air supply completely. "Why are you afraid of me, Julienne?"

She made a last-ditch effort to muster a scathing look that should have cut him dead. But it didn't. Her heart wasn't in it. "You seem to have all the answers."

"No, I've got a lot more questions about you than answers." He let go of her hands and lightly touched her hair. There was gold mixed in with the deep, dark color. It fascinated him. All of her fascinated him. "And I'd really like the answers."

"I'm afraid you're going to have to keep on wondering." She moved her head back slightly, but seemed utterly unable to rise to her feet again. "Why do you insist on playing with my hair?"

"Because it feels so silky."

"Please stop." Any moment her eyes were going to flutter shut, drifting with the sensations he was creating. "I don't want you to do that."

"Look me in the eye and say that." The challenge was softly worded and incredibly seductive.

"I . . . I—" The words, the denial, wouldn't come. "Oh, damn you."

"Maybe. But it'll be worth it." He cupped the back of her head, tilting her face up to his. His mouth found hers again, and once more he felt the desperate sweetness that was there, the needs, the loneliness that she kept imprisoned within her. It stirred him, aroused him and made him ache. He pulled her up until she was on the sofa next to him, her body leaning into his.

Over and over again his lips touched hers, taking just enough to sustain him, giving just enough to make her want more. It cost him, but he kept his passion bridled just enough not to frighten her. He had to be very careful not to lose himself in her, in the hot, fiery well that her kiss opened up for him.

He felt her respond and yet he couldn't help feeling that there was more, that she was resisting, holding back a part of herself. He wanted that part. He wanted all of her.

She meant to push him away. With every ounce of her being she meant to push as hard and as far as she could, but her hands were betraying her, clutching the front of his shirt, curling into the fabric, feeling the warm skin that was just beneath. One second, just one second to feel this way again, she promised herself, and then she could break free.

Again? There had never been a first time. It had never been this powerful before, this utterly breathtaking. It was as if her whole being was reduced to a pulsating, yearning core.

With a moan J.T. pulled away. She couldn't let this happen to her. She felt disoriented, dazed. She pressed her palms to her cheeks, certain they were burning. Everything inside her was quivering. "I don't think you should do that again."

"I do." His eyes on hers, he took her hands and moved them away from her face. He refused to let her look away. "Julienne, I'm not going to do anything you don't want me to."

She shook her head. "Not good enough."

"Why?"

"You know why." Because you'll make me want things I have no business wanting, she thought in despair. Things that'll make me yearn for a world that doesn't exist. I won't be hurt again. I won't.

He saw the mounting pain in her eyes. "Maybe I do at that. But I promise you we'll take it slowly. Very slowly."

She pulled her hands free and got up, moving away from him. "Why don't you go back to your bricks or your boards or whatever and—and build something?" she cried in desperation, just wanting him to leave.

"I thought I already was." Because there was fear in her eyes he backed away. "But there is some work I left unfinished at the office so that I could take a spin in the solar system today. Maybe I'd better be on my way."

"Um, don't forget your duffel bag." She nodded at the floor.

"Right." He swept up the bag and swung it over his shoulder.

Because manners were as much a part of her life as breathing, J.T. accompanied Shad to the door. She wasn't certain if she did it because she wanted to be sure to shut the door on him, or because she wanted the luxury of a few extra moments with him without the fear. Right now she wasn't certain of anything.

"Thanks for the meal." He stopped at the door. "It was excellent and, believe me, I was raised on food that was out of this world."

"Your mother's?" She bit her lower lip, realizing her mistake.

"Foster mother," he corrected easily. "See you at the science fair." He closed the door behind him.

She leaned against it, letting out a long breath. How could being orphaned not faze him? she wondered. He bore no scars, showed no pain. He seemed a lot happier, a lot better adjusted than she was, and she had had her natural parents and Adriana. And why was he doing all this, being so nice to her son? Was he unconsciously repaying some sort of debt because someone had taken him in when he needed a man's influence?

He left her wondering about a lot of things. Mostly about herself and how she was going to survive another one of his visits. She had barely made it through this one. She needed a shower, a long one. She needed to stand and let the water hit her until both her body and her mind were numb. Then maybe, just maybe, she'd be able to bury what Shad had stirred within her.

She was afraid. Afraid to let go, and almost as afraid not to.

As she made her way to her room, J.T. passed Frankie's bedroom. She stopped because the door was open. Frankie's door was never open these days. Heartened, she peered in. Her flippant, devil-may-care son was sitting, slouched in a chair, his feet dangling over one side. The boy was actually reading.

Frankie looked up, sensing his mother's presence. "Is he gone?"

J.T. nodded.

Frankie's smooth, young face furrowed in disappointment. "I thought maybe he'd stay a little longer."

"Why? You're the one he came over to help."

"I know, but I thought that maybe he'd..." Frankie's voice trailed off.

J.T. crossed the threshold and stepped into the blue-and-white room. "What? That he'd what?" She couldn't begin to guess what was on Frankie's mind.

Frankie lowered his eyes to the book, his voice sullen. "Never mind. I'm just getting to the good part."

J.T. nodded. "See you in the morning. Sleep well."

Frankie raised his eyes tentatively, about to say something, then obviously thinking better of it. "You, too, Mom."

Well, at least they had had a semblance of a conversation, J.T. thought, walking into her own room. That was hopeful. She supposed she had Shad to thank for that, too. The plus marks on his tally were mounting. Too bad she knew that ultimately they didn't mean anything. It would have been nice to believe that they did, if only for a little while. But that would have been foolish. And she was through with being a fool.

J.T. sought out the comfort of her shower.

By the time Friday arrived J.T. was firmly convinced that her original assessment had been right. Shad was like all men, quick to give his word, and just as quick to forget it. There had been no calls from him, no suggestions of meeting under some pretext. Nothing. She berated herself for having, even for an instant, gotten caught up in the merry-go-round ride he had offered. This time she was too smart to buy a ticket. She wasn't twenty anymore. Or naive. Not her. She told herself that the gnawing sense of disappointment she was experiencing was for Frankie—by proxy.

Because she had promised, and because she knew that any tenuous headway she had made with Frankie would be lost if she didn't come, J.T. arrived at Frankie's school a quarter after three, just in time for the science fair. It hadn't been easy to arrange this free time. She'd had to reshuffle her schedule, and some of her clients hadn't liked that. But clients didn't mean anywhere near as much to her as Frankie did.

The gym was alive with young voices full of anticipation and hopeful parents giving projects last-minute scrutiny. For a moment J.T. didn't think she could find Frankie in this crowd. But then she saw her son over in the corner, his expression carefully constructed to appear that he didn't care if he was alone, his eyes darting from side to side, searching.

J.T. made her way through the throng to reach Frankie. "Hi!" J.T. wove her arm round the boy's shoulders and gave him a little squeeze.

Frankie looked up, but the bright smile that flashed across his face faded a little, to be taken over by one of surprise. "You came." It was both a question and a breathless statement.

"I said I would," J.T. told him, knowing that hadn't been enough other times. In the past few months their relationship was littered with promises that hadn't been kept because of emergencies that had arisen at the last minute. Never again, J.T. promised herself. No matter what it took she was going to be there for Frankie. Shad had been right about saying that she was losing Frankie in the shuffle. Providing for him physically had taken precedent over emotional support. Never again.

J.T. saw the way Frankie continued to search through the crowd. "Honey," she said softly, "I really wouldn't build up my hopes. He probably forgot." The bastard, she added silently, wishing she could give him a good, swift kick.

Frankie refused to listen. "But he said he'd give it his best shot."

"And he probably did." She couldn't believe she was actually defending him. "But, well, you know how these things are."

"Yeah." The hurt in the bright blue eyes was difficult to ignore. "You gave me a lot of practice."

No, this wasn't going to dissolve into a conflict. "I know, but I'm here now."

A cutting retort seemed to tremble on Frankie's lips, but then he smiled slowly and relaxed. "Yes, you are." He squeezed his mother's hand.

Relieved, J.T. put her arm around her son's shoulders. "C'mon, let's have a look at these projects."

Frankie was more than willing to take her on a tour, pointing out ones he thought he could beat, and the ones that would provide stiff competition. They stopped at his model. J.T. slowly walked around it, studying it from all angles. It was good. Very good. And she wasn't just thinking that because it was her son's, she thought defensively. It really *was* good.

"I think it looks terrific," she told Frankie.

Frankie glowed. "I did it pretty much myself, you know." He shoved his hands into his back pockets and rocked slightly on the balls of his feet. "Shad told me I had to, so that when it won, I could feel really proud of it." He turned his face up to J.T. "He's pretty neat, huh, Mom?"

There was no getting around it. At least not for Frankie. "Yes, I suppose he is."

"Thank you."

J.T. swung around, her heart lurching. He was here. He'd heard her, damn him. Why had he come sneaking up like that? She had already made up her mind to stay aloof when and if he came. How could she do that when he had just heard her praise him?

"You came!" Frankie exclaimed excitedly.

"I gave you my word, remember?" He scanned the other projects, assessing their chances. "The bidding went over."

"Bidding?" Damn, he got her again, she thought. She had promised herself not to show any interest in anything he said.

"On that new mall that's supposed to go up next spring in Malibu." He crossed his arms over his chest, studying their project.

She had read about the proposed mall. "You're bidding on that?" She had thought of him as a small-time contractor, someone who answered his own phone and maybe got by picking up odd jobs like fixing garages. This put another light on the subject.

"Not anymore." He grinned, thinking of the pleasure he had felt when the project had been awarded to his company. "We got it." He looked around. "Is there a phone someplace?"

"There's one at the pizzeria down the road," Frankie told him.

"Good, we'll go there to celebrate after you win." He winked at Frankie. "I have to call Angie about the contract."

"Angie?" J.T. repeated the name without realizing it. He was going to call a woman to share the joy with her. But he had said he was unattached. Of course, that was last week. Someone like him didn't stay that way for long.

J.T. had no idea she had allowed her disappointment to show.

Shad saw the look entering J.T.'s eyes. For a moment he thought of fueling it to make her realize that what was going on between them *was* going on between them and that it wasn't just one-sided. But he had never been one for games. "He hates when I call him that."

"He?"

"Boy," he said, looking around the gym, "this place has some echo." Then he looked at J.T., who, he thought, looked as if she was about to strangle him. "My partner. Angelo Marino. But I've been calling him Angie ever since we were kids."

She tried to look annoyed, but the relief she felt wouldn't let her. Angie was a man. "You seem to like calling people by names they don't like."

"Yeah." A committee of three stopped at a nearby table. "Shh, here they come." He crossed his fingers elaborately for Frankie's sake.

"How did you know they were the judges?" Frankie asked, puzzled.

"Easy," he told him in a low voice. "They're not smiling. They think that if they smile, maybe someone will think they're not taking this seriously."

"Gee, you know everything." There was unabashed admiration in Frankie's voice.

"Almost everything."

J.T. groaned audibly.

"I said almost," he whispered in her ear. His warm breath tickled her skin. She couldn't help smiling in response.

They watched as the solemn-looking trio drew closer. Two women followed closely behind a white-bearded man who nodded and conferred with his committee, then made notes on his clipboard and walked on, passing Frankie's model.

"That's it?" Frankie watched them walk by, disappointed.

"They have to look at all of them," Shad pointed out.

Frankie barely nodded, watching the judges with wide hopeful eyes.

Finally it was over. With fanfare that stretched the proceedings to an intolerable limit for the participants, the judges announced their choices. Frankie took third prize. He was ecstatic.

He held his trophy before him and allowed his mother to hug him. Frankie's smile was wide, but it grew a little wistful around the edges. J.T. saw it, but Shad was the one who commented.

"What's the matter, Frank?"

"Nothing..." he said quickly, then lowered his eyes.

"But?" he prodded gently.

"Well," he said, stretching out the word, taking a deep breath, "I would have liked first."

"Everybody would have liked first. Third isn't shabby," Shad pointed out, affectionately ruffling his hair. "Next year we'll take first."

"Next year?" Frankie echoed, anticipation already taking hold. "All right!" He raced over to share this with one of his friends. J.T. hung back with Shad, glaring at him.

He was aware of her displeasure, but not the cause of it. He watched as Frankie pointed toward him for his friend's benefit. He was glowing.

"How could you?"

Shad looked at J.T. in surprise. "How could I what?"

"How could you have promised him next year?" It was hard to keep her voice down.

How could he do that? How could he lie like that? Who knew where he would be next year? Certainly not here. Why should he be? There were no ties for him, no attachments. The words were easy for him to toss off. Didn't he understand that Frankie believed him? That he would be heartbroken when he didn't keep his word?

"Because it's in my power to promise that, Julienne."

"Promise? You have no idea where you're going to be a year from now," she said between clenched teeth.

"Oh, I think I do." The look he gave her was meaningful.

J.T. had no idea what to make of it and was afraid to try. But she couldn't stop the smile that rose to her lips as Shad ushered the two of them out of the building.

"Next stop," Shad announced, "the pizzeria."

The man was crazy, absolutely, positively crazy. What was worse, she was fighting an overwhelming desire to take a ride on a merry-go-round.

Chapter Eight

The pizzeria was dimly lit, crowded and noisy. Everyone at the science fair, it seemed, had had the same idea they had. Off in the corner was a wide-screen TV tuned to a baseball game that was being played out somewhere in the country. Every so often Frankie would devote several seconds of attention to it, getting completely involved and then tearing himself free just as quickly and bringing his enthusiasm back to the subject of the science project, school, Shad, everything and anything. Frankie was his old self again, happy, animated.

Because of Shad.

It was all because of Shad. Try as she might to stop it, the soft spot in J.T.'s heart was widening. He had managed to do with Frankie in a very short time what she, for all her good intentions, couldn't. She owed him.

It made wanting to be rid of him very, very difficult.

But his very presence, the very thing he was doing for Frankie, was creating feelings within J.T., worse, *dreams* that had no place in her life anymore. She had gone that path before, clinging to a hope, a man, who ultimately failed her. It wasn't even his fault. It was, she knew, just the way things were. They were only different in those programs Norma loved so dearly. No wonder the housekeeper watched them with such rapt attention. But J.T. had to continue to make her way in the real world. The real world was no place for dreams.

Shad spun the large pizza tray toward J.T., bringing the last slice to a halt before her and interrupting her thoughts. He raised an eyebrow slightly.

J.T. shook her head in answer to his silent question. "If I eat that, the next sound you hear will be me, exploding."

"You had your chance." Shad picked up the slice, anticipating it with as much relish as he had the first.

There was something very much the small boy about him, J.T. thought, amused. He attacked everything in life with gusto, as if he wasn't aware of the disappointments that were just around every corner. But he had said he was orphaned at a young age. Then he knew all about life's grim side. How could he be like this? It was just in his nature, she decided, just as it was in his nature to continue the cycle he undoubtedly felt was started by his foster father. She knew Shad wasn't about to be Frankie's foster parent, but for a while he would give the boy the kind of warmth and attention he had received himself.

She watched as he made short work of the slice. Frankie, sitting on her right, was absorbed in something called a double play happening between the two teams on the screen. Shad had had five slices if her count was correct.

"Where do you put it all?" The man didn't look as if he had an ounce of fat on him, just muscle, an inordinate amount of sculpted muscle. Probably had something to do with his line of work.

"I don't." He wiped his mouth and let the napkin drop on his plate. He looked almost wistfully at the empty tray. "I burn it up." He looked at them inquisitively. "Can I offer you two anything else?"

Frankie shook his head. "I'm stuffed."

"A forklift would be nice," J.T. muttered. A lethargic sensation she was unacquainted with inched its way through her body as she rose to her feet. She normally didn't eat until dinner. If she had anything at all during the day, it usually consisted of some sort of fruit drink that her secretary had mixed for her at the local health food bar around the corner from her office.

Shad shook his head, amused. She had had exactly one and a half slices of pizza, nibbling at them slowly while he and Frankie had practically devoured the rest. Dedicated dieters could model their lives after this woman. "Lady, you have a long way to go before you'd ever need one of those. Right now you look as if you need to keep bricks in your pockets in a stiff wind."

"Are you telling me I'm too thin?" She remembered his comment at the game when he tried to tempt her with a hot dog. He had called her skinny that time. She glanced at Frankie's broad grin. The boy appeared more interested in watching them than the game on TV. "He is, isn't he?" She was flirting, J.T. thought suddenly. And liking it. This had to stop.

A little later.

"He's a minor." Shad came to Frankie's defense before the boy could agree. "He's not allowed to get involved in these kinds of discussions. And you're not too thin," he observed. "You're perfect."

Why should such a simple compliment, totally untrue though it was, reduce the chemical composition of her knees to water?

Shad's chair scraped against the floor, creating a swirling path in the sawdust. "Time to go, I guess."

As always, Shad positioned himself between them and took each by the arm, guiding them through the noisy pizza parlor. This time it felt less awkward to J.T. It felt right, which frightened her. She tried to resist but felt herself relaxing despite her best efforts. Maybe he had drugged the pizza.

She glanced at her son. Frankie's face was lit up like a Christmas tree. It was the kind of look she had always wanted for him. It was the kind of look a boy wore when he having a good time with his family. With his father. She wished she could give Frankie that. A father who would look out for him, who would make him feel the way a boy should. Who could open up the world for him and show him the good things.

Small chance of that, she thought ruefully. Pete had completely disappeared from their lives without a trace.

J.T. pressed her lips together, guilt gnawing at her. She hadn't even been able to give Frankie a full-time mother lately, much less a father. She guessed she should be grateful to this unexpected fairy godfather, whatever his origins and however long he stayed in their lives. At least he was making Frankie happy, and because of him she had made the time to come to the science fair and share in Frankie's moment. J.T. couldn't lie to herself. If it hadn't been for Shad, she would have probably never known about the science fair to begin with. Frankie wouldn't have told her.

It was all going to change, J.T. promised herself again. Thanks to him.

She looked at Shad intently as he held the door open for them. How long *would* he stay in their lives? she wondered. She didn't want to lose this feeling, this glow for Frankie. And, if she was being honest, she didn't want to lose this feeling herself, either. Not yet. She knew she was being frivolous, but it *did* feel nice, sharing things like this, like a family. The way she had always envisioned sharing things with Pete and Frankie. And before that with her own parents.

Shad saw the wistful look that entered J.T.'s eyes as they came out of the pizza parlor. It was amazing how the woman's eyes changed, growing darker, lighter as thoughts filtered through her. He could read her emotions as they ebbed and flowed. She probably wouldn't make a very good poker player.

"Something wrong?"

His voice was low, intimate, as if he really cared. She knew it was just an illusion, yet still . . .

She shook herself free of the wish. It was Frankie she was supposed to be concerned about.

"I was just wondering..." Hesitating, J.T. ran the tip of her tongue along the outline of her mouth. It strummed a chord within Shad. Desire vibrated, strong and demanding. He curbed it as best he could, promising himself a time when it wouldn't have to be curbed.

There were street noises around them, cars moving, people hurrying to their destinations, yet she was aware of silence as both Frankie and Shad waited for her to finish speaking. As if they knew this was hard for her.

"I don't suppose you do small jobs anymore, what with this mall contract and all." What was the matter with her? She was practically stuttering. She, who could always speak so well, hiding her inadequacies behind precise, cool rhetoric. She balanced hundreds of thousands of dollars daily in various account books. She went to meetings with heads of large companies. She was competent, respected. But right now she sounded like some vacant-headed teenager.

"That depends." He led them to his car. "What did you have in mind?" He knew he was just drawing out the conversation. Whatever she had in mind, he'd find the time, even if meant inventing another seven hours in the day and learning how to operate on automatic pilot. He liked being with them, with her. Any excuse that came his way he'd use. "An addition?"

"No, nothing that ambitious." Her palms felt damp and she wanted to wipe them. She clenched her hands at her sides instead. "That is—I need the bathroom remodeled."

"I see."

She saw the look in his eyes. He saw, all right. He saw this as a pitch by her to keep him in Frankie's life—in their lives. In hers. She tried to save face. "Maybe you could recommend someone who might—" She almost walked right past his car when he took hold of her arm, stopping her. She felt like an idiot.

"I could do it." He played with a strand of her hair. She had worn it down. On purpose? he wondered. He'd like to think she had.

Out of the corner of her eye she saw Frankie watching them. What was he thinking? Did he feel shut out? Did he—?

J.T. cleared her throat, pushing on. "Mainly I'd like Frankie's enlarged. An enclosed shower stall put in." The words tumbled out faster. "And different tile, maybe—"

He tossed Frankie his keys and he opened the door, hitting the automatic switch that unlocked the others. With a grin that seemed far older than his years, he made himself comfortable. In the back seat.

Shad turned back to J.T. "You don't have to do this, you know."

"I don't?" She saw the look in his eyes. Was he laughing at her? Did he feel sorry for her? Damn him, anyway.

She was an idiot to have started this. But there was no graceful way to back out. "On the contrary, I've been wanting to redo the bathrooms for the past six years. The timing's never been right, that's all. First, I had to finish getting my degree, then set up the business and money was tight—"

"Okay." He placed a gentling hand on her shoulder to stop her before she verbally raced off any further. "Whatever you say." He saw through it, but let her have her pride. Pride, he knew, was a very important commodity. "Why don't we talk over the details tonight? Over dinner."

"Dinner?" Her eyes were large, startled. Almost frightened, he thought.

"Dinner," he repeated.

She looked over her shoulder at the pizzeria. "I don't think I could ever eat again."

"You will. Trust me." He leaned into the car and looked at Frankie. "That okay with you, Frankie, my taking your mother out?"

Frankie was both startled and then pleased at being consulted. The slow glow that came into his eyes said that he'd like nothing more. "Sure, Shad. But she's a cheap date."

"Francis!"

Frankie peered out, looking a little sheepish. "Well, you never eat much."

Shad was taking obvious pleasure in the exchange, J.T. thought. "That means I get to finish your meal." He held the door open for her and J.T. slid in.

She watched him as he got in on his side. "You really love to eat, don't you?"

He drove away from the curb, taking them back to the school parking lot a short distance away. "Passionately. It's right up there in my top two vices."

''What's the other?'' she heard herself asking as he brought the car to a stop next to hers.

''We'll discuss that, too. Eventually.''

As she and Frankie transferred to her car, leaving Shad behind, J.T. had a rather uneasy feeling that they would.

''Eight all right with you?'' he asked before she had a chance to flee. ''For dinner, I mean.''

She nodded, then started the car, needing to get away, needing to breathe air that wasn't filled with the scent of his cologne. For a change Frankie chattered as they drove home, and J.T. forced herself to get lost in her son's words.

Damn, she couldn't believe she was letting this happen to her. Eight o'clock was approaching with frightening speed, and she still hadn't gotten ready. Dating was for the birds, she thought, for teenagers who had the stamina for it. What was it her secretary called it? ''Socializing'' that was the term for people who were out of their teens. Well, she didn't feel out of her teens, not tonight. She had never had much practice at this, anyway. She had married the first person she had gone out with.

Idiot.

She wasn't sure if she was applying the term to herself or to Shad.

Shad.

The muscles in her stomach began to quiver again. Sure, he was cute. Sure, Frankie liked him, but that wasn't enough of a reason to get involved. That wasn't enough of a reason to risk getting hurt, even remotely. So what was she doing, fixing her hair, putting on her favorite blue cocktail dress to discuss tile? What could he possibly tell her over dinner that he couldn't tell her over the phone? Or at least in her own house—with Norma and Frankie close by, acting as chaperones?

"You don't need a chaperone," she said aloud to the mirror. "You're a big girl now, remember? You've come a long way from that frightened, insecure woman Pete left behind."

If that was true, why were her insides trembling like this? And why didn't the image in the mirror look even vaguely convinced?

She had no answer. But she did have a solution. She was going to call Shad and cancel. That was what she was going to do. She didn't need this. She had enough things crowding her life. She . . . heard the doorbell ring.

"Oh, God."

Her hand flew to her stomach, just as it lurched. She had purposely kept men at a distance since her divorce. That part of her life was over. It was utterly unnerving, anyway. She might be able to make sharp judgment calls when it came to business, but she was lousy at sizing up a lifetime partner, and that was where, as far as she was concerned, any relationship was supposed to go.

Oh, Lord, she wished he'd go away. She wished she could just tell him that she'd changed her mind. What could she have possibly been thinking of this afternoon? She must be going crazy. Stress, that was it. She was having a stress reaction.

"He's here!" Frankie bellowed up the stairs. "Hurry, Mom!"

J.T. leaned her palms on the bureau, bracing herself. "Famous last words." She looked at the open window. No time for a fast getaway. With her luck his car was parked right beneath her bedroom window, anyway. She took a deep breath, told herself it was only for a few hours and just about business.

Here goes nothing, she thought.

* * *

Shad stood at the foot of the stairs, watching as J.T. descended.

The reason for his attraction rammed home. Dressed in a muted blue dress that came in at her incredibly small waist, flowing out gently on hips that begged for his hands, J.T. looked like something that had walked out of a dream. His dream. He hadn't realized he had been waiting for her all his life until he saw her just like that. She took his breath away.

"Hey." Mysteriously he had found his voice. "You look terrific."

Her hand felt damp on the banister as she clutched it. She descended slowly, afraid that as she decreased the distance between them, she was walking into something she had absolutely no control over.

Now. Tell him you can't go out now, before it's too late. "Shad, I—"

"Can't wait to start talking about the renovations, I know." He took her arm, not possessively, but firmly enough to let her know the decision to flee had been taken away from her. "But I thought we'd hold back until the waiter brings our cocktails. So we'd better be on our way." He turned toward Frankie, who stood, his hands linked around the banister, watching. The boy was a good study, he thought, and was undoubtedly making notes. "I'll have her back before midnight, sir."

Frankie grinned. "You can keep her out later than that if you want."

"Translation," Shad said knowingly, "you want to watch TV, right?"

Frankie's grin grew broader.

"Fair enough." He saw the look of protest enter J.T.'s eyes. He was quick to block it. "I think that, in honor of coming in third in the science competition, he should have an extra privilege, don't you?''

J.T. knew when she was outnumbered and outmaneuvered. She gave up. "Why should I have anything to say about it? I'm just the mother."

"There's no such thing as *just* the mother. Is it okay?" Shad pressed.

She knew she had been manipulated, but couldn't help liking him for appearing to give her the final say. J.T. smiled at Frankie. "It's okay."

Frankie gave her a quick, impulsive hug. "Thanks, Mom." He let go. "You two have an awesome time, okay?"

She could have sworn she heard a hopeful note in Frankie's voice. Oh, no, not you, too, she thought with a flash of despair.

"How do you keep doing that?" J.T. asked as they walked out to his car.

"Doing what?" He moved around to the passenger side and held the door open for her.

J.T. sat down and her skirt rose, making her wish she had worn a longer dress. The feeling was heightened when she saw the appreciative look in Shad's eye. He shut the door for her. "Manipulate things so that Frankie and I wind up on a better footing?"

"It's a gift," he said lightly as he pulled the car out of the driveway. Natural instinct had a lot to do with it, too, he thought. A part of him had always sworn that if he ever had a family, he'd do things right. The thought that perhaps he was in this relationship for the wrong reasons flashed through his mind. Was he being goaded on because he had always *wanted* to be part of a family? He wasn't sure anymore.

He stopped at the lights at the end of the block. "Mexican all right with you?"

He had chosen her favorite type of food. "Mexican is *always* all right with me." She forced herself to settle back in the seat. This would be less painful if she relaxed. "Was that a lucky guess?"

"Actually, no. Frankie mentioned it to me."

"Out of the blue?"

"Yes." He turned a corner. "Right after I asked him what sort of food you liked."

She laughed, shaking her head. "You don't leave much to chance, do you?"

The flow of traffic was almost nonexistent. The restaurant he had chosen was only two miles away in the center of a mini-mall. "On the contrary, some things I do. Other things are too important to."

"Like dinner?"

He turned to look at her for only a moment. But it was enough. "Like you."

J.T. forced down the lump in her throat and stared straight ahead. "I don't think I understand."

He turned into the restaurant's parking lot. "I think you do."

Desperation clawed within her. She didn't believe in making the same mistake twice. She wouldn't let herself make it twice. "Shad, this is just to discuss renovations. On my house," she said with emphasis, knowing that if she didn't qualify her statement, he'd start talking about making other "renovations" in her life.

He took her arm. "If you say so."

J.T. let out a short, bedeviled breath. "You could drive a person crazy, you know that?"

"I'm working on it."

J.T. stifled a scream.

The restaurant looked like the re-creation of a Mexican cantina. The tile beneath their feet was wide and bronze, echoing their footsteps as they followed the gaily dressed hostess to their table. Off to the left three mariachi players were meandering from table to table, playing tunes that were softly melodic. Romantic.

"Is this table all right?" the hostess asked Shad.

The table was in the heart of the restaurant. He raised an eyebrow, looking at J.T. Surprised that he deferred to her, J.T. looked around and saw a table nestled off in the shadows. "Is that one taken?"

"No." Obligingly the woman escorted them to that one instead.

Shad waited until the hostess had given them menus and drifted away. "Afraid someone will see you here with me?"

J.T. opened the tall green menu and pretended to scan it. Letters swam in front of her without meaning. "No, of course not."

"Afraid to be seen having a good time?"

She looked up. "Why are you analyzing this?"

"I want to learn everything about you, Julienne."

His smile was easy. So easy to get lost in. J.T. held her ground. "I really wish you'd stop calling me that."

"Why?" He put his hand over hers and felt it stiffen. He kept it where it was, slowly rubbing the soft skin with his thumb. "I think it's a lovely name."

He was making her nerve endings do things she didn't want them to. He was making her feel things she didn't want to. "That's not the point."

"What *is* the point?"

"Your calling me Julienne is too personal."

"I mean to get personal, Julienne."

"Don't."

The soft background music framed his words. "Too late."

She put down the menu. Disaster. She was poised on the edge of disaster and she was about to fall over. But not without a fight. "Then turn back the clock, because I'm not the one for you."

"Why don't you let me decide that?"

"I appreciate everything you've done for Frankie—"

He wouldn't let her lie, even to herself. "We're not discussing Frankie. We're discussing his mother."

Please, please stop. I don't want this to be happening. "His mother is a woman who doesn't want to get involved with anyone at the moment. At *any* moment."

"How long have you been divorced?" he asked quietly.

She didn't like talking about her divorce. It brought memories back. "Eight years."

"That's a long time to brood."

J.T. raised her chin. "I'm *not* brooding."

"Okay, I'm trying to feel my way around here. Help me out." He leaned forward. "What are you doing?"

He was making this so difficult for her. She didn't want to let him in. "Trying to fend you off."

"Why? Do you find me irritating?"

"No."

"Repulsive?" he guessed.

"Of course not," she said emphatically, then cleared her throat. "I mean, no."

Being a gentleman, he suppressed his grin. A little. "Then what?"

"You're a man."

"I can't argue that point. But that's what makes the relationship fun." She looked down at her hands. He reached for hers, and she pulled back, but he wouldn't let her. "Tell me, Julienne," he coaxed.

The eyes that looked up at him were large, luminous. And filled with pain. "He promised me forever and a half." A sad smile played on her lips. "He didn't even stay for the half." She looked off into the darkness. The music somehow made the moment even more melancholy. "He just got restless," she whispered.

Anger twisted his insides, anger at a faceless man who had caused her so much pain. "Just because he couldn't handle it isn't any reason to write off the species as a whole, Julienne."

She pulled back her hand, squaring her shoulders. Why wouldn't he let it go? "I can't go through all that again, putting my feelings on the line, hoping I'm not wrong. Hoping the wind doesn't shift, taking him with it."

"Not all men are afraid of commitment, Julienne. Some look their entire lives for it."

"Ready to order?" the waitress asked brightly, oblivious to the scene she had intruded upon.

"Yes, I think we are. Julienne?"

Mechanically J.T. placed her order, grateful for the respite, but knowing it was just temporary. Shad wasn't going to go away that easily. He'd stay. Until she became used to him. And then, then, she'd have pieces to put together again. When he left.

She'd done it once. She could do it again. Maybe it got easier the second time around. But she doubted it.

Chapter Nine

"You're kidding, right? Tell me you're kidding," Angelo implored.

Shad sat at his desk, doing a last-minute calculation on the computer. Angelo was always quick to flare up before he calmed down and approached things logically. Shad had seen it happen over and over again. By now he was immune to the outburst of emotion and hardly glanced in the shorter man's direction as he spoke.

"If I told you that, then I'd be lying to you, Angie, and I've never lied to you." He rubbed his chin, absorbed in the problem on the screen.

Angelo put down the order forms that Sandra, the secretary they both shared, had pressed into his hands as he'd passed her on his way into Shad's office. "Oh, no? Well, how about that time in high school when you convinced my date I was sick and I—?"

"Okay, once." Shad held up a finger, stopping Angelo as he waited for the computer to give him the answer he was looking for. Angelo edged closer to look over his shoulder. Shad sighed, satisfaction washing over him as the right answer appeared. It was going to work out just as he had thought it was.

"We'll discuss your qualifications for the George Washington award some other time. Right now I want to know why you suddenly get it into your head to play Mr. Handyman. That was Pop's thing, working just with tile and bathrooms. You were the one who came in like gangbusters and made us expand, remember?" Angelo threw up his hands in frustration. "Now you're reverting back just when we've got a mall to build."

"Oversee," Shad corrected, hitting a key that brought up another screen. The bare design began to fill with colors and took on a three-dimensional appearance. Pleased with what he saw, he leaned back and looked in Angelo's direction. "Most of that is in the way of supervising. You're up to doing that on your own for a couple of weeks, Ange. I know you are. The drawings have all been approved, the suppliers contacted. And we've got the manpower to go ahead with it on schedule."

Angelo leaned back until he was partially sitting on a corner of Shad's desk. "Is that how long this affair of the heart is going to take you—a couple of weeks?"

"No, that's how long the bathrooms are going to take. The other, I can't quite say."

Angelo crossed his arms on his chest. "Level with me, Shad. Is it serious?"

Shad stored the program before he turned in the swivel chair and faced Angelo. He knew Angelo was asking out of concern. Over the past twenty years they had shared a lot together, tears, triumphs, dreams. More than most brothers. "I think so."

"So what does this lady have that the others didn't?"

A smile played on Shad's lips as he thought of J.T. She was beautiful, but that wasn't enough. There was a kindred spirit beneath the unconscious, appealing sensuality that called to him. That needed him. "Sad eyes."

"So do I when you say you want to play hooky from the business. I don't see you falling all over yourself for me."

"You're too ugly." Shad laughed. He pressed the print button on the keyboard, and the wide-carriage printer snapped to life, whining and grinding as the multicolored ribbon reproduced the structure Shad had finished creating only moments ago.

Angelo glanced at the finished drawing emerging out of the printer and grunted his approval. "So when do I meet her?"

Shad shut off the computer and printer, then turned to his large spiral notebook. The top drawing was of the changes he had drawn for J.T.'s downstairs bathroom. "The lady is very, very skittish. It might take a while." He eyed Angelo, as if appraising him and finding him wanting. "It might take a long while."

Brilliantly white, even teeth were a contrast to the dark golden hue of Angelo's complexion. "Afraid I might steal her from you?"

"Afraid she'll take one look, think genes might be transferred by proximity and head for the hills." Shad made a notation of the type of fixtures he wanted to use and pulled over the card file to find the right supplier's phone number.

Picking up the pad, Angelo looked over the sketch of the redesigned bathroom. "Not bad. Every bit as good as Pop's." He handed the pad back to Shad. "I might even hire you myself."

Shad let the cover fall back on the pad. "I'm too expensive for you."

"Don't I know it." Angelo gave Shad an affectionate cuff on the ear. "Well, if all you're going to do is sit around on your duff, mooning, I'd better get these order forms to the supplier. One of us has to work." He pulled open the door.

"Tell me how you like it for a change," Shad called after him.

Angelo waved a hand at Shad in dismissal, then poked his head back in a moment later. "Good luck, little brother."

Shad grinned, nodding his head. "Thanks. This time I might need it."

"I don't want anything too extravagant," J.T. warned, looking over the blueprints later that afternoon. They had only gone over the idea of renovations on Friday. Here he was on her doorstep Monday evening, drawings, tile samples and catalogs in hand. He worked fast. Too fast, she thought, the customary nervousness that accompanied his presence wafting through her.

She looked down at the pages spread out on the dining room table. The precisely measured lines meant nothing to her, but they looked intimidating. She didn't have that much money to spend on this impulse of hers. But the thought of backing out wasn't a viable alternative. A week ago it would have been; now she couldn't seem to form the words.

"I just wanted them modernized. New cabinets, colored faucets, things like that." She knew she sounded vague, but she wasn't really certain what it was she wanted—other than having Shad come by a little longer under a safe pretext.

"That's all I've done." He tapped the top drawing.

J.T. looked down at them again, this time really studying the drawings. "You do these?"

She was still skittish around him, he thought. It was going to take time to get her to trust him. He only hoped he'd have the patience. "My computer picked my brain."

"Your brain does good work," she murmured, always able to appreciate good workmanship.

She was surprised, though, that she could concentrate at all. Having him here, even with the breadth of the dining room table between them, still made her nervous.

"Something I learned from my foster father." He took the drawings from her, their hands touching in the transfer. The current was there, suppressed. Waiting. It was only a matter of time. "It was his business," Shad went on as if he hadn't felt anything, as if he didn't want to take her into his arms and kiss her until they were both senseless. "He was a skilled laborer, a master tile man. After I got out of school, Angelo and I expanded the business to include additions and houses."

There were a hundred other things she should be doing rather than sitting here, discussing renovations she really didn't need and hadn't thought of until last Friday. Yet she couldn't make herself get up and leave. Her legs wouldn't work. "And malls."

Fruitlessly she searched her mind for something more to say. She preferred the nervous energy of rapid chatter to the sensual stillness of his eyes. When he smiled like that, all she could think of was touching those lips to hers.

Why did this have to be happening to her again? she thought in pure anguish. She knew what to expect. She had been there already. The trip could be fun, but arriving was awful. Common sense should have told her not to want him so much. Common sense had taken a holiday.

"This is our first," he admitted. He took a sip of coffee, thinking he didn't need an additional stimulant. "Angelo's nervous enough to have kittens."

"Then shouldn't you be working on it with him?" It was as close as she could come to telling him to get out of her life. Because she no longer wanted him to go.

He knew what she was doing and it hadn't a prayer of working. "It's good for his confidence to go some of the distance alone."

J.T. thought of all the things she had had to face on her own. It would have been wonderful to have someone to lean on, someone to turn to. Her fingers tightened around the coffee cup. "Maybe."

"Was it frightening for you?" he asked quietly. "Going the distance alone?"

"Terrifying." Her head jerked up as she realized what she had just admitted. "I mean—"

He put his hand over hers. "There's no shame in being human."

She would have liked to have left her hand there, warm, protected. But she knew things like that were just illusions. At least for her. "There's no percentage in it, either." She pulled her hand away and looked at her watch. "How soon can you get started?"

"Tomorrow morning." He gathered the drawings together neatly. The scent of her perfume, exotic, elusive, like her, filled his senses. "You're always looking at your watch."

"Sorry, habit." She was careful not to look at him. He seemed to be able to read things in her eyes, things she was so certain she kept secret. "My time is always so limited."

"Clocking yourself limits you even more."

She blinked. "What?"

"You can't have a sense of infinity if it's broken up into tiny pieces."

An ironic smile lifted one corner of her mouth. "Minored in philosophy, did you?"

"No. In life. Actually, I majored in it. Mostly against my will at first. Kind of like you."

She stiffened. "There's no comparison between—"

"Our lives?" he finished for her. "Oh, I think there is." He returned the drawings and catalogs to his portfolio and carefully zipped it up. And though his manner was laid-back, his eyes held her fastened in place. "I know what it means to feel you're not wanted. To feel there has to be something in you that was lacking, that drove the other person away." Right now he bore a lot of animosity toward a man he had never met for wounding her this way, for making it so hard for him to explore what there might be between them. "But that's not always true, you know. Sometimes people do things that have nothing to do with you, even though they wind up hurting you. Your husband left you because he was a coward."

J.T. opened her mouth to protest, but what was the use? It was true. Hadn't she thought of Pete in the same terms? Lying awake in the early hours of the morning, hadn't she labeled him the same way? Still, she was a private person, and this invasion of her thoughts, her feelings, made her angry.

"He was a coward," Shad repeated, "because he couldn't face life. My father left my mother and us for much the same reason, so I'm told."

His voice was so impersonal, so matter-of-fact. Didn't he feel anything? Everything else about him was so full of life, so lusty when it came to living. Why was this piece so different? Was this his way of handling the torment that never left? she wondered. She forgot to be annoyed at his intrusion. Suddenly there were things she wanted to know about him, about his pain.

"And your mother?" she asked in a whisper.

Unlike her, his gaze didn't drop. He looked into her eyes as he answered. There was nothing to be ashamed of, nothing to apologize for. Things were the way they were. And he had managed to survive them. And prosper. "Died. From something as simple as the flu. I was eight. Dottie was five."

She could see him then, lost, alone. Protective of his little sister. It was then that a tiny bud of pure affection burst open, flowering in the shadows of her heart. It was completely against her will, but that didn't seem to matter. "And there wasn't a relative, someone to take you in?"

"The court never found anyone." He thought back, remembering the fear, the loneliness. The awful weight of responsibility. Dottie had been so afraid. And so had he. "There were, in the first years, a few families that were willing to adopt us. Separately. But we wouldn't be separated. So they farmed us out to foster homes."

"That must have been awful."

"Some of it." He shrugged carelessly. "The rest was average. Until Salvator Marino took us in."

Fondness flooded through him as he recalled the first time he had ever seen the man. On his knees, setting tile. He had stood in the doorway, an unsure, defensive boy of eleven. Salvator had let him stand there for a few minutes before motioning him to his side. Shad had started helping Salvator the first day. And his self-esteem had started to rebuild.

"God, there was a man. He made up for everything that happened before. Big, lusty, always looking at the possibilities life offered. Even in the worst of times. He always saw the positive side. I've always wanted to give back a little of what he gave me."

And that's why you're here, she thought. She shut away the sadness that created within her. J.T. broke off a piece of the pound cake Norma had baked that afternoon during *Family Ties*. But her appetite was gone. "But he didn't adopt you?"

Shad shook his head. "Couldn't. Some kind of hang-up about age and money. He was too old to be our father and didn't earn enough money, according to the social service requirements. But he wasn't too old to be our foster father. He knew a few people—everyone loved Salvator—and pulled a few strings. He managed to get us to stay with him for over six years. By then I was eighteen and could go wherever I chose. I chose to stay with him."

Shad was quiet for a moment. They both heard the muffled dialogue from the television in the kitchen. "So, now that you have my whole life story, and I have bits and pieces of yours, I'd say we're ready to create a bathroom together." His eyes twinkled and he put out his hand. "What d'you say?"

She slipped her hand into his. His grip warmed her. It was the hand of a strong man, a man circumstances hadn't bent to their will. "It's a deal, McClellan."

He hadn't won her over completely. He knew that. But some of the guarded look in her eyes had vanished. It was a start.

It surprised J.T. that instead of coming with a group of workmen, Shad worked alone. He arrived early, in time to see J.T. rush off to the office. He stayed all day, often conferring with Norma about what to serve for dinner that night.

And soon it was all too easy to get used to him being there.

He sent J.T. on her way with a wink and a wave and made her look forward to coming home again. Frankie enjoyed coming home to him. More than once, by the time

J.T. got home, she'd find work in the bathroom abandoned and Shad and Frankie in the backyard, working on the boy's pitching arm. If Shad was working, she'd find Frankie with him, either acting as his assistant, or sitting cross-legged on the floor, struggling through his homework and occasionally shooting questions at Shad that he answered thoughtfully.

Frankie was changing right before her eyes, thanks to him. He was happy, contented. The edge that had set them at odds these past few months was gone.

The edge was gone from her, as well, J T. mused as she stood just outside her son's bathroom, watching the two of them work together. Shad was replacing the tile inside the newly installed shower stall. Or rather, Frankie was replacing it under his careful supervision.

It was Shad who sensed her first and looked over his shoulder, still keeping one eye on what Frankie was doing. He could always sense her presence. It had become second nature to him now.

"Home kind of early, aren't you?" He knew she was. How quickly he had committed her habits to memory. He wanted to think she had come home early because of him. "A little to the left with that one," he counseled Frankie, his hand hovering just above the boy's, not touching but ready to assist if necessary.

J.T. shifted a little, like a schoolboy caught playing hooky. "I took your advice."

Shad grinned over his shoulder. It sent a shiver like white lightning zipping along J.T.'s spine. "Which advice was that?"

"About delegating responsibilities. I'm letting Rafferty handle the new account."

Whatever it took to make her come home. "Fine man, Rafferty."

"Alice Rafferty is a woman," J.T. corrected, knowing Shad had no idea who she was talking about.

"Fine woman, Rafferty," he repeated without skipping a beat.

She laughed. He was always so unruffled, even when he made mistakes. "Doesn't anything throw you, Mc-Clellan?"

He leaned his shoulder against a section of wall that hadn't been stripped yet. "The sight of a beautiful woman coming home early from work, observing her handsome son become a master tile setter does."

"Handsome?" Frankie stopped and looked up at his mentor. "Me? Ha. Jenny Samuels says I look like a duck."

He was grinning, but Shad knew the comparison had stung Frankie. "Jenny Samuels is in desperate need of an ophthalmologist."

Frankie started to laugh, his hand shaking as he held the tile just above the place he was inserting the light blue squares.

"You'll laugh when I say so," Shad instructed, pulling his grin into a serious expression for exactly half a beat. He straightened the tile Frankie had placed by a fraction of an inch. "There, now you can laugh. We're finished for the day," he pronounced, stepping out of the shower. Frankie followed him out. "Dinner, anyone?"

J.T. shook her head, amused. "Don't you think of anything else except food?"

He eyed her for a moment, his look deep and penetrating. "Yes."

J.T. turned before the sudden, unbidden blush spreading out over every inch of her face. "I'll see if Norma's ready yet," she said briskly. "You'll join us, of course."

"Of course." He rolled down the cuffs of his shirt. "You're having London Broil tonight."

"London Broil?" That wasn't what she had told Norma to serve. "But I thought—"

Shad led the way out of the bedroom. "Norma wanted to know my favorite."

"Why didn't you just say food and make it simple?" J.T. asked. She went off to find Norma and see what went on in her kitchen while she was away at work.

"So, have you decided if you're going to the dance yet?" Shad asked Frankie at the table.

Both mother and son looked at him in surprise. It was the first that J.T. had heard of a dance. It wasn't something that she thought Frankie would be interested in. To her surprise, a guarded look came over Frankie's face. The way it used to.

"How did you know about that?" Frankie asked.

"I overheard you talking to your friend on the phone when I brought the supplies into your bathroom the other day."

He was getting too entrenched in their lives, J.T. thought, waiting for Frankie to answer. He knew more about her son than she did. He changed menus, helped solve math problems and brought chaos and order at the same time. What was she going to do about him? What *could* she do about him?

And what was she ever going to do without him?

Frankie lowered his eyes and stared at the last piece of steak on his plate. "No."

"Can't dance?" Shad asked casually. He was well aware of teenage insecurities. His memory of his own teen years was excellent, and he had had the added stigma of not having natural parents.

Frankie shrugged and mumbled, "I can dance as well as any of them."

Shad knew by the way he answered that he didn't dance. But there was more than that stopping him. "Then why don't you go?" he prodded gently.

J.T. came to his defense. "Shad, I think Frankie can make up his own mind whether or not he's going." J.T. remembered how terribly awkward she had always felt at the dances she had had to attend during school hours. They had been so painful for her. Her shyness had been seen as aloofness, and she had been shunned. She didn't want the same thing for Frankie.

"I know that," he said easily. He turned his eyes on Frankie. "I was just curious about his reasons."

Frankie gulped down his milk before answering. "Dances are dumb."

"Sometimes," he agreed. "But they're also a way for people to get together who otherwise might not."

J.T. expected Frankie to give some sort of flippant answer and then bolt from the table. Instead, he mumbled, "What if you don't get together?"

"You mean if no one wants to dance with you?" Shad asked knowingly.

Frankie leaned his face on his knuckles, dejected. "Yeah."

"I think you'll have the exact opposite problem."

"Aw, you're just saying that." But the look in his eyes took on a hopeful, pleased note, urging Shad on to convince him he was wrong.

He was going to be dynamite when he got older, Shad thought. "No, I'm being honest," he answered simply. "I've got eyes, Frankie. And beneath that baseball cap is a pretty good-looking guy that a lot of girls will want to dance with and go out with."

Frankie laughed, but he wasn't totally convinced. Twelve was the age of immense hope and despair. "But what if they ignore me?"

"They won't," J.T. said. Frankie looked at her in surprise. It was her own firm belief that her son was going to be a heartbreaker one day. He already had the looks for it. "I guarantee it. Although I think that everyone should be a wallflower at least once in their lives."

"A wallflower?" Frankie echoed in disgust, trying hard to understand and failing. "Why?"

"Because being a wallflower teaches people to be humble and kind. Besides, it's not the worst thing in the world. You know what is?"

"What?" If Frankie hadn't asked, Shad would have. He found J.T.'s philosophy infinitely more interesting than dinner.

"Being insensitive to other people and their feelings," she said quietly.

For a moment there was silence, then Shad leaned over toward her. "You going to eat that?" he asked J.T., intentionally breaking the mood.

J.T. looked down at her plate. True to form, she had left a little less than half her steak. "No."

He took her plate and replaced his own empty one with it. "Thanks."

"I think Norma might propose marriage to you soon," J.T. warned, watching. "She loves to see someone clean their plate."

He continued to eat with gusto. "Always glad to help out when I can."

"Well, eat fast," J.T. urged, impulsively making up her mind. "Because after dinner I'm going to give Frankie a few brushup lessons on dancing."

Frankie frowned, but didn't protest. It was a very heartening sign, J.T. thought.

"You got it." Shad retired his utensils and pushed the plate away.

Yes, J.T. thought. I've got it. At least for now.

Chapter Ten

Frankie followed Shad and his mother into the family room, looking rather doubtful again about the entire proposition. Insecurities resurfaced. "But what if no one says yes if I ask them to dance?"

"Then," Shad told him calmly in the tone of one adult speaking to another, "you talk to the other guys and still have a good time."

Frankie stuck his hands into his back pockets. "I can stay home and do that."

Shad placed his hands on Frankie's shoulders. The gesture was both supportive and firm. "You should always leave yourself open to new experiences. Life has a lot to offer if you're not afraid to take a chance." He looked over Frankie's head at J.T. "A lot to offer." Dropping his hands, he stepped back. "I believe the floor is yours, Julienne."

She saw the uncertain, defensive look in Frankie's eyes. Taking a deep breath, she moved forward. "I want you to pretend that I'm one of the girls at the dance."

Frankie laughed in disbelief. "You?"

Shad moved back, a grin on his face. He tried to imagine what she would have been like when she was around Frankie's age. Delicate, shy. He wished he could have known her then.

"Me." She nodded, placing one arm around Frankie's shoulders and huddling. "Now I'm going to let you in on a secret, Frankie." She lowered her voice conspiratorially. "Very few guys your age have ever been privy to the kind of thoughts that go through a girl's mind at a dance, but because you're my son, I'm going to make an exception. As long as you promise not to tell anyone. Promise?"

Shad coughed in his effort to stifle a laugh. But Frankie was completely taken in. "What? What?"

"Okay. Now I'm the girl." Stepping away, she began to create the scene, gathering memories to her. She struck a casual, nonchalant pose, but her agitation was evident in the way she twisted the handkerchief in her hand.

Frankie started to laugh. J.T. momentarily abandoned her pose. "Hey, don't laugh. I'm supposed to be the cream of the crop, okay?" Those were the words her father had used, she remembered. He hadn't meant it as a compliment. It had been her duty to reach that level. The hurt he had generated was something she had always promised herself she wouldn't inflict on her own child. "Okay, now I'm going to let you hear what's going on in my head. Ready?"

Frankie and Shad exchanged looks. "Ready," they chorused in unison, then they all laughed. J.T.'s heart felt full. When was the last time they had laughed together like this? It seemed like an eternity ago.

Norma, drawn by the laughter, forgot about the show playing on her set and edged over into the family room to watch.

The scene set, J.T. pretended to notice Frankie for the first time. Shad could almost swear she *looked* like an adolescent girl, awkward, nervous and struggling oh-so hard to look nonchalant. Could she have been this painfully insecure as a teenager?

J.T.'s eyes opened wide as she looked in Frankie's direction. "Wow, look at that guy." She straightened, tossing her head so that her hair shook, taking on a free, wild look. "Maybe I should kind of go over and—naaah." Her shoulders sagged a little. "He'll never ask me to dance. He's too cute."

"I am not." Frankie took a step forward.

J.T. held up her hand, stopping him. "Shh. You're not supposed to be a mind reader." Lowering her head, J.T. was back in character. She looked around restlessly. "Maybe I should've just stayed at home." She sighed, pulling some of her memories to her. "But I had to come. The other girls would think I'm just a bookworm if I didn't show up." Then, while Frankie stared at her, J.T. straightened, her body tense.

"Hey, he's looking this way. He's coming over. Oh." She moaned. "I hope my palms aren't sweaty." She looked down at them, embarrassed. "They are. They are sweaty. Boy, if I take his hand now, he'll slide right out of the gym and into the street."

J.T. ignored the laughter that met her remark. She rubbed her hands on the back of her skirt, anticipation etched on her face. For a moment she was reliving her own past, her own insecurities, the ones she had hoped to leave behind when she fell in love. But they had only multiplied. Shad watched, utterly fascinated.

"What if I make a mistake?" J.T. was debating, her indecision painfully obvious in her stance, the way she held her head. "What if he doesn't like me?" The thought appeared to be devastating. "Hey, I can't handle rejection." She looked over her shoulder. Panic entered her voice. "The girls are watching. Maybe I'll just walk away, very coollike, and get something to drink before he gets here— Too late." Her voice rose, cracking. "He's here." J.T. looked at Frankie and beckoned. "That's your cue, Frankie," she whispered.

Frankie bit his lower lip uncertainly. "What?"

She held her hands out to him. "You're going to take pity on a nervous teenage girl and dance with her."

"But there's no music." Frankie looked around, as if it were a tangible object he could see.

"In your head, Frankie." J.T. smiled softly at her son. "In your head. A slow dance."

Frankie's eyes grew even wider. Without realizing it he had been pulled into the little drama J.T. had created. "Slow?"

He wasn't all that different from her, J.T. thought affectionately. "Don't jump out of your skin. Here's how it's done." She positioned him so that he was comfortable. Her hands resting lightly in his, J.T. looked down into Frankie's face. "Now we're back in this girl's mind, okay?"

"Okay."

Slowly they moved around the floor, J.T. guiding him effortlessly. Frankie began to get the hang of it and grinned broadly. J.T. grinned back.

"I wonder how I'm doing," J.T. murmured, back in character. "He hasn't tried to excuse himself. That's a good sign. Wish my palms would stop sweating. Wish *I'd* stop sweating. Gee, this song's a long one. Hope I don't step on his feet before it's over. Hope it doesn't end too soon. I like having him hold me.''

She smiled, the tenseness in her body relaxing a little as a revelation struck. "Hey, this isn't so bad. I think I've even stopped sweating. Sort of."

J.T. stopped and looked into Frankie's face. "There, see? The girl at the dance is just as afraid as you."

Frankie debated for a second. "I think she's more afraid."

"Probably." J.T. glanced in Shad's direction. Behind him she saw Norma hustling back out to her kitchen and undoubtedly another show, she thought. But the woman was smiling and nodding her approval as she left. "So what do you think? Think you can live through it?"

Frankie's chin went up as his eyes danced, his confidence abounding. "Piece of cake."

"That's my guy." J.T. laughed, giving him a quick one-armed hug.

Frankie wiggled free. "I've gotta call Karl and tell him we're going to the dance. He won't go without me," the boy confided to Shad.

"You're the brave one, huh?"

"Yeah." He didn't even see the humor in Shad's eyes as he ran off.

"Have you ever thought of stand-up comedy?"

Shad's voice was low and sexy as he asked the question. J.T. struggled for control as she felt herself reacting to him. "Too busy," she said lightly.

J.T. felt suddenly restless. There was something, some flame, some passion that leaped into life each time they were alone together. She could curse it, him, herself, but she couldn't deny it was there any more than she could stop it from being.

"That was a very nice thing you just did."

"He's my son."

"For some people that's not enough of a reason to lay their souls bare." His eyes were making love to her, melting her where she stood, even though he hadn't laid a hand on her.

"I didn't." The words were hardly a whisper. He saw through her, she thought. There was no use in protesting.

He took a step toward her. "Dance?" He held out his hands.

Unconsciously imitating her son, she looked around. "But there's no music."

"In your head, Julienne. In your head," he repeated the words she had used softly, waiting.

There was no retreating. Nor did she really want to. Taking a fortifying breath, J.T. stepped into his arms. It was a little frightening at first, being so close to him, feeling the rise and fall of his chest, the heat of his skin as it permeated hers. Frightening. Exhilarating.

It was like coming home.

"Just relax," he coaxed, whispering the words into her hair. Gently he pressed the small of her back, swaying slowly and dancing to music only he could hear.

On the perimeter of his consciousness he was aware of a squeak as the kitchen door was cracked open. Norma was peeking in again. She grinned, gave him the high sign and withdrew to her sanctuary. But this time the sound of the television set wasn't heard coming through the wall. Norma was trying to create an atmosphere, Shad guessed, and blessed her.

"Easy for you to say," J.T. murmured.

"What?"

"Relax," she repeated, her cheek against his chest. The musky smell of his skin sent excitement tingling through her. Age-old desires rose, demanding fulfillment, reminding her she was a woman who needed love.

"Actually, yes," he agreed, then tilted her head slightly so that he could look into her eyes. "Easy for me to say. Not easy for me to do, though."

He confused her. "I don't understand."

Shad pressed her hand against his chest, covering it with his own as they continued to sway in place slowly. She could feel his heartbeat. His hips molded against hers in a gentle, yet erotic movement. "You know that scenario you just re-created for Frankie?"

"Yes?"

"Well, it's not exactly limited to people who still have trouble deciding which acne medicine to use."

He couldn't possibly be saying what she thought he was saying. "You're not trying to tell me that you lack confidence?"

He nodded. She couldn't tell if he was teasing or not. "Right now I'm trembling in my shoes."

"Yeah, I'll bet." If he lacked confidence, then she was Wonder Woman.

"Sure I am." His smile faded slightly as his eyes grew serious. "I'm afraid you'll reject me."

She could only dully repeat the word. "Reject?" She didn't think in terms of his being rejected. Only her.

"Yes, when I do this."

She saw it coming. From a mile away she knew she had seen it coming. Maybe she had even willed it to come. Because once his lips touched hers she knew she had been aching for this moment to happen again, counting moments since the last time he had kissed her. Like some uncertain, love-struck teenager who didn't know what lay ahead. Except that she did. She'd been there before, hands filled with dreams, only to have them scattered and destroyed like so many snowflakes in the morning sun.

And yet . . .

And yet she wanted to kiss him. Like an obstinate child who knew something was wrong and yet did it, anyway, she wanted this, wanted to feel his arms around her, his mouth on hers, his body against hers.

She wanted to make love with him.

No.

Needs and wants fought with the sobriety of common sense, pulling her in opposite directions. If she was to survive, she had to stop this. But what price survival?

A moment more. Just one moment more.

J.T. threaded her fingers through his hair, her body leaning into his. Fire licked all through her, making her head spin, disorienting her. Her breath caught in her throat until she didn't think she could ever breathe again, ever want to breathe again away from him. His tastes were dark and deep and manly and she couldn't get enough.

She felt so small, so delicate, Shad had to remind himself to be gentle for fear she'd break right here in his arms. His passion was so great that it would have been easy to let it overwhelm them both. But he knew he couldn't let it. Not just because of a housekeeper in the other room and a young boy upstairs. But because of Julienne. He had to teach her to bend, not break. To run toward, not run from.

The passions that vibrated within him each time he kissed her reinforced how much he wanted her. And how much he swore to himself that eventually he'd have her. Willingly. Not through seduction, not through the hunger brought on by abstinence. But with her eyes and heart opened, opened to what he could offer.

J.T. placed her hands on his shoulders and pushed him back, breaking free. She couldn't do this, couldn't let even this little ground go. She had made a mistake once, and one mistake was one too many when the stakes were this high. He seemed wonderful. But once, so had Pete. She didn't trust her own instincts, not when it came to men. Memories of her failed marriage rose up to haunt her.

"Shad, I can't." Her words came out in a breathless rush.

"You just did."

"You know what I mean."

"No, you're going to have to tell me."

"Shad, you don't understand—"

"Then explain it to me."

She moved toward the window and looked out, afraid that if she looked at him, she'd break down. And above all else she had to maintain her control. It was all that had seen her through the last time, built up bit by bit from nothing. It was still so frail. Maybe it would always be.

She leaned her palms on the windowsill to support her shaky limbs. She saw him watching her in the reflection, his image merging with that of the solid old oak tree in the front yard.

"I married Pete when I was very young. I thought he was the most wonderful man who had ever walked the face of the earth. I was very naive."

He touched the ends of her hair. He wanted to hold her, but knew she needed space. How much longer he could give it to her, he wasn't sure. "That's no crime."

"He was so vital, so exciting, so full of life. And I couldn't match him."

What she was implying made him angry. "What do you mean, 'match him'?"

She shrugged, too embarrassed to continue. "Maybe I'd better stop—"

"No, you started this. I'd like to hear you out." He turned her around to face him.

Her head jerked up, hurt and anger in her eyes. "I wasn't woman enough for him, all right? He said I didn't satisfy him."

How could she be so stupid? "Maybe he just wasn't man enough to do it right—to appreciate you. Part of all this is making your partner enjoy what's happening. It's not supposed to be one-sided. He was wrong, Julienne." Shad placed his hands on her arms lightly to keep her from fleeing. "You're more than enough of a woman for any man." Ever so gently he ran his finger along her bottom lip. "And he was a fool to have walked away from someone like you. But if he ever tries to return to rectify his mistake, he's going to have me to face."

She wanted to believe him, to believe that it was going to be all right. He made it sound so simple. "You really do know how to say the right things, don't you?"

"I don't know about the 'right' things, Julienne." Shad leaned his head against hers. "But I can tell you what's in my heart. I'm not sure where this road is leading us, but I know I have to take the road and follow it to the end."

Filling his hands with her hair, he lowered his mouth to hers again, knowing he would never get enough and that one taste would make him only want more. In the distance they heard the phone ring insistently.

"Mr. McClellan, it's for you. A Mr. Marino." Norma peeked in from the kitchen, the long beige telephone cord twisted around her arm, the receiver aloft in her hand. "He claims it's urgent." Her tone told him she didn't think anything short of an earthquake was urgent at this moment.

"I gave Angelo and Dottie your number," Shad explained to J.T., reluctantly releasing her. "In case they needed to find me."

J.T. touched her lips with her fingers, nodding. Saved by the bell, she thought wryly. Another moment and she would have drowned completely in his kiss.

There were worse ways to go, she mused.

Shad took the receiver from Norma, absently nodding his thanks. Norma huffed, withdrawing. It was obvious what she thought of this interruption. He tried to keep his impatience out of his own voice. Angelo's timing could have been better. "McClellan."

"We're missing some of the inventory at the site, Shad. I'd really appreciate it if you could get your tail over here for a few hours."

Shad ran his hand over the back of his neck, thinking. He had called over to the site yesterday afternoon. The foreman had assured him then that everything was all right. Obviously something wasn't. "You there now?"

"Yes."

"I'm on my way." Shad hung up. "I'm afraid I'm going to have to go. It can't be helped."

J.T. nodded. Actually, it was for the best, she thought. She had bared too much of her soul. She needed time to regroup.

Shad could read her thoughts in her eyes. She was slipping away again. Damn. For every two steps forward he slid one back. Still, Shad knew the full value of patience. Lifting her chin in his hand, he kissed her lightly on the lips.

"To be continued," he promised.

"Shad, maybe—"

"I'd better get to the site before Angelo has heart failure. Yes, you're absolutely right."

She opened her mouth to protest that that wasn't what she was about to say, then stopped, grinning. He was impossible. Maybe that was what she liked about him.

And maybe there was a whole lot more to it than that.

Shad had a feeling that the trouble at the site wasn't going to be solved within a few hours. It looked like his weekend would be shot.

"Listen, I'll see you Monday. If you want to talk, you know where to reach me."

"Yes, I know." Monday seemed suddenly so far away, yet she needed the time, the distance, to clear her mind. It felt so muddled right now that sometimes she couldn't remember what was best for her.

Somehow, though, she couldn't bring herself to let him go. She strung together bits of conversation. "I've got accounts to see to." She was babbling. He knew she had accounts to work on. That was all she ever seemed to be doing—working on accounts.

He caught the inflection in her voice and realized she was trying to tell him that she was going to miss him. Another step forward.

He ran the back of his hand along her cheek, loving the feel of her. "Frankie told me he really wanted to see that new action movie that came out on video this week. I think that might be a better way to spend the evening, don't you?"

She glanced at the VCR. When was the last time she had watched anything at all, let alone with Frankie? Too long. The boy's name made her smile. Shad had gotten her used to calling her son by his nickname. He had made a lot of changes in her life in such a short while. "Maybe you're right," she agreed.

"Of course I am. It's in your contract. Read the fine print." He slid the back of his hand along her cheek. "Check it out."

"I will." She closed the door and let herself smile. "Frankie," she called out.

In a moment the boy was shouting from the top of the stairs. "Yeah, Mom?"

"I'm going to the video store to rent *Murphy and Malloy*. Wanna come along?"

Frankie took the stairs down two at a time, his startled expression giving way to a large, pleased grin. "Hey, you bet!"

"Well, c'mon. Time's wasting." J.T. put her arm out and slipped it around Frankie's shoulders as the two of them went out.

Chapter Eleven

It seemed to J.T. that everything that could have gone wrong *did* go wrong. It started with the alarm failing to go off in time. She slept away an extra twenty minutes, time that was precious to her. When she did wake up, she hit the floor running, trying to catch up.

"I'm late," she said in answer to Norma's accusing look as she grabbed the cup of coffee from her place at the table and ignored the rest of the food.

She tried not to look in Shad's direction. She knew what he was thinking. No matter how late she was she should sit down and have something to eat. No doubt it went along with his smell-the-flowers theory. Today, though, the flowers had to be put on hold. She had a meeting with a Mr. Jacobs, who was thinking of changing to her firm.

Draining the cup, she sneaked a look at Shad. Shad was sitting opposite Frankie at the table. It occurred to J.T. even as she rushed that she had gotten very used to seeing him wandering around the house, poking his nose into things, being part of their lives. It had all happened so quickly.

How was she ever going to adjust to *not* seeing him when the time came for him to move on?

"Bye, honey." She kissed the top of Frankie's head, noting with no small pleasure that the boy no longer pulled away. "Have a good day."

"You, too, Mom," Frankie called after her.

Score one for the home team, J.T. thought happily as she rushed out.

"One day she's going to wake up and see that life's passed her by while she was working on some account or other that in the long run doesn't matter a hill of beans," Norma complained loudly as she placed Shad's coffee in front of him.

"I heard that!" J.T. yelled from the front door as she checked her briefcase for the last time.

"Good!" Norma retorted.

Her day went downhill after that.

Maybe it was Norma's comment about always rushing around, dealing with things that eventually wouldn't matter, that finally hit home and nagged at her. Or maybe it was the fear of not seeing Shad anymore once the work on the bathrooms was done.

Whatever it was, J.T. couldn't seem to concentrate and function at her usual level. Murphy's Law saw to it that she was confronted with one emergency on the heels of another. The meeting with Jacobs could have gone better. She came away with only a definite "maybe."

The headache she had been nursing since she sprang out of bed was growing.

By one o'clock J.T. was ready to call it a year, much less a day. The last straw came when the office temp, who was taking the firm's secretary's place for what appeared to be two endlessly agonizing weeks, spilled her mug of coffee. On J.T.

It was an omen, J.T. decided. Someone or something didn't want her working today. Who was she to argue?

With the young woman's apologies following her all the way out the door, J.T., her skirt soaked, left the office and headed for home and sanctuary.

She muttered under her breath all the way from her Costa Mesa office, her irritability mounting as the miles to her house decreased. Not only had Jacobs not come around the way she had hoped, but they had just lost another important account because the owner's nephew had emerged this month out of graduate school, waving a degree in accounting in his hand. The owner wanted to "keep things in the family." So it was either marry him, she thought wryly, or lose the account. She lost the account.

She pressed her lips together. J.T. hated losing an account. It brought back all those awful, insecure feelings she had when she first got started in her business. Losing clients made her very nervous. It not only put her future in jeopardy, but more importantly, Frankie's. How was she going to afford the best colleges and grad school for her son if her clients were leaving in droves?

J.T. blinked back an angry tear. She had to get hold of herself before her emotions got the better of her. Bringing her car to an abrupt halt in the driveway, she got out, slamming the door in her wake. It made her feel a little better.

Norma's car was missing, which meant she was at the market. Just as well. In her present mood, J.T. thought, she'd probably take the woman's head off for a wrong word. And there were times when Norma was full of wrong words. Since Shad had appeared, Norma kept dropping blatant hints that J.T. should throw a lasso around him and run to the nearest minister. Unlike sitcoms, she thought, jamming her key into the lock, life didn't have a happy ending.

The house was muggy. Outside, it was unseasonably humid, especially for June.

"It figures," J.T. muttered.

It was the kind of day best suited for crawling into bed and pulling the covers over her head. Except that it was much too hot for that, even if she were so inclined.

The weather seemed to hang solidly in the air, a barrier of heat to overcome. With an impatient sigh J.T. marched into the family room and turned on the air-conditioning unit. An unearthly screech shattered the stillness, making her jump. The high-pitched noise reminded her that she had neglected to call the air-conditioning man for a long-overdue maintenance check.

Murphy's Law again.

Everything was conspiring against her.

She raised her fingertips to the grating, praying for a whoosh of cold air. Warm air continued to swirl around her hand. Wanting to cry, J.T. let her hand drop. She was now bordering on total irrationality, but that didn't change matters. It was the kind of day when even a hangnail would have probably reduced her to tears.

Unconsciously she glanced down at her hands, expecting to see broken nails. Finding none—yet, she amended, taking no news well—she trudged up the stairs, unbuttoning her blouse as she went. She wondered how long she should wait before calling Jacobs back again.

Reaching the doorway of her bedroom, she took off her jacket and tossed it carelessly onto the bed. A kaleidoscope of thoughts dashing through her mind, she began unzipping her skirt as she entered. She stopped, glancing down. A huge, jagged pattern of brown spread out over the white linen.

"Hopeless," she muttered.

The coffee stains would probably never come out. Why should they? Nothing had gone right yet. The Emery account was overdue, the Wiley account gone and the temp was still having trouble learning the alphabet. Why should anything go right ever again?

"I wouldn't do that if I were you—unless, of course, you're prepared to suffer the consequences."

J.T. jerked, her hand grabbing her skirt, which was past her hips, on its way to the floor and exposing the bottom half of what looked like a very enticing teddy from where Shad stood.

Sucking in her breath, J.T. swung around and looked at Shad accusingly. He was down on his knees in her bathroom, and right now grinning very broadly.

"What are you doing in here?"

"Working." He held up the tool in his hand as proof. "That was the arrangement, remember?"

She remembered very little at that moment beyond her name. Because of the heat Shad had stripped off his shirt long ago. A sheen of sweat coated the hard muscles, making J.T.'s mouth suddenly turn to cotton. He was gorgeous, absolutely, positively gorgeous. The muscles in his shoulders and arms seemed to ripple seductively as he rose to his feet. J.T. reminded herself that breathing was a necessary process for sustaining life-forms, and she should be doing it.

As an afterthought, she yanked up her skirt, zipped it closed and hastily tucked in her half-unbuttoned blouse. It didn't help. She felt exposed, totally exposed, and not a little aroused.

He ran his hand through his hair. It was damp, but heat never bothered him. She, however, did. "Anything wrong?"

"Nothing." Unconsciously, because survival was an ingrained instinct, she took a step back. "Nothing at all."

"You looked frazzled." He had never seen her looking worse. Disheveled was kind of cute on her, though he didn't think she'd appreciate the observation. "And what happened to your skirt?"

She looked down at it dumbly to remind herself. "Betsy tripped."

"Betsy?"

"The temp at the office. She was carrying her coffee cup around at the time."

He winced at the thought of the scene that must have transpired. "Is she still alive?"

"What's that supposed to mean?" J.T. asked defensively. She wasn't an ogre, though she felt like one at the moment. An overstimulated ogre.

"You don't look very friendly."

"I don't feel very friendly," she admitted, then eyed him as he bent down to retrieve another tool from the huge toolbox that lay open on the floor. "Are you making fun of me?"

He caught the vulnerable, testy edge in her voice. "No, I'm not stupid. I like living." Carefully using half turns, he tightened one of the two screws at the base of the toilet with a wrench, then secured the decorative cover. "Why don't you change and turn on the air conditioner? I think you need to cool off."

"I did," she snapped, not taking kindly to the criticism.

He looked at her over his shoulder. "This is cooled off?"

"No." She pushed her hair out of her eyes. She should have worn it up. It was just that . . .

Just that he liked it down, she thought, placing the blame on him. It was his fault she felt like this. All his fault. "I turned on the air conditioner. That was the screech you probably heard. It died."

"I'll take a look at it after I finish with this." He nodded at the toilet tank. It was pearl-gray, a pleasing contrast to the dusty-rose tile he had spent the past two days installing along the wall. Here and there a single flowered tile was intermixed with the solid pink.

"I'd thought you'd be done in here by now." That was why she hadn't bothered looking in when she had entered. He was so fast that subconsciously she had just assumed he was working on the downstairs bathroom by now. Frankie's had taken him only four days.

"The tank gave me trouble."

"Oh?" She noticed an innocuous slim black clip sticking up on the ball cock joint inside the tank. "What's this thing for?"

He glanced over his shoulder. "Don't!"

The word was hardly out of his mouth when her fingertip came in contact with the clip, sending it flying in a jet-propelled arch through the air. It was immediately followed by a geyser of water that shot up to the ceiling, ricocheted from there and within seconds drenched them both. A sudden summer shower was now coming down full force in her newly decorated bathroom.

J.T. screamed as water hit her face with the force of a fire hose. Her mouth filled with water and she started coughing. Groping to get out of the line of fire, she stumbled backward into Shad and sent him sprawling into the soaked rug. She landed on top of him. Even in the frenzied situation, with water gathering around them, the instantaneous reaction flaring between them, hot and demanding, couldn't be missed.

Reluctantly pushing her to one side, Shad quickly reached for the faucet behind the tank to shut off the water. It wouldn't budge. He had tightened it too hard earlier. With water gushing up and out at an incredible volume, Shad rifled through his toolbox for a pipe wrench. Finding it, he gripped the faucet in the tool's teeth and applied force. The faucet finally turned and the water stopped.

Letting out a long breath, Shad sat back on his heels, water dripping from every part of his face and body. "The clip," he said calmly, as if the flash flood hadn't just engulfed them, "keeps the water pressure from shooting out."

He dropped the wrench and looked at J.T. She was in the middle of the bathroom, her hair plastered to her face, her skirt plastered against her body and her body plastered against the submerged rug. "So much for ever making you my assistant."

J.T. stared at him. And then she started to laugh. At first a little, and then so hard that she couldn't sit up straight. The frustration and helplessness she had felt gave way to laughter, totally cleansing her. She nearly fell backward, and Shad made a grab for her, her laughter infecting him. They fell over and landed on the floor again, laughter echoing in the room, their bodies tangled together.

And then the laughter died abruptly as other, stronger emotions suddenly took over.

With water clinging to her lashes and her hair, she looked like the embodiment of a mermaid. She was the most desirable woman he had ever seen. Needs hammered through him, harder, even harder than before. His mouth closed over hers, savoring, taking, giving. Driven by an achingly sweet desire, he kissed her cheeks, her lips, her eyes.

Abandoning herself to him, J.T. slid her hands up his back, holding him to her as the almost overwhelming desire she imprisoned within her broke free. Reactions slammed through her body, made that much more intense by the passions, the frustrations that had been held in check over the past few days.

The floor, the water, the events that had led up to this moment were all forgotten; everything was forgotten except the needs that raged within, the needs Shad had held back for her sake. The needs she had repressed these past eight years, needs that had been born within her so long ago, never to be satisfied.

He tasted her lips, her throat, the swell of her breasts that rose just above her teddy. She arched toward him, greedily savoring all he had to give. His pulse throbbed, creating a rushing noise in his ears. It felt as if all control was gone. He wanted to touch her everywhere, to feel her against him, know what it was like to taste all her special flavors.

For one moment it seemed that he would burst the bonds that restricted them both. It seemed so easy, so tempting. So right. He had wanted her from the first moment he had seen her, but never as much as now. They were alone in the house. . . .

But for how long? At any moment Norma could return from the store. Or Frankie could come home unexpectedly. After all, hadn't Julienne?

He couldn't risk it. Not for her sake, even though he felt as if he would die if he didn't have her.

Slowly, achingly, he rolled off her.

"We'd better not get carried away. Norma's due back any minute." He touched her face, tracing the delicate contours as if to seal them forever in his mind. Her pupils were huge and she looked slightly dazed. It made him smile. No more than he. "I feel a little like a dolphin."

With effort she caught her breath, gratitude and disappointment warring within her. What kind of man was this?

To bring her to the point where she would have willingly given in to her feelings and then to back away because they might be discovered. Her body ached, missing the pressure of his.

He was nothing like Pete. Pete would have taken her right then and there, and damn the consequences. He wouldn't have been thoughtful, wouldn't have put her feelings above his own wants.

God, she loved him. What was she going to do about that? What in the world was she going to do?

She looked at Shad, trying to shake her dazed feeling. Hesitantly she brushed the hair from his forehead. "You don't look like a dolphin," she murmured with a sad smile.

You don't look like someone who'll break my heart, either, she added silently, but you will.

He rose and offered her his hand. There were still huge drops cascading down the walls and pink tile. Water was absolutely everywhere. A large drop fell onto his head from the ceiling. Beneath his feet water puddled on the thick rug. "Can I make a suggestion?"

She surveyed the situation, dismayed. "Anything."

"Let me install tile on your floor."

"Do I have a choice?"

"Sure." He picked up the dripping toolbox and put it on the counter. "You can go with tile, or you can live with the smell of a wet rug for about a week or so."

"Tile wins. How soon can you have it here?"

He couldn't resist. Pulling her into his arms, his body molding against hers, he brushed the wet hair out of her face, marking the trail with his lips. "Well, just because I like you, I'm going to make you a deal you just can't refuse. I can have the tile here tomorrow. How's that?"

"Terrific." And the word, she thought, applied to more than just the deal.

"You two building an indoor swimming pool?"

They turned in unison to see Norma standing in the bedroom, her usually fluffy white hair wilting around her face.

Shad laughed, releasing J.T. "It wasn't anything we planned."

Norma's hands rested on her wide hips. "Neither was the lake in the kitchen, I take it?"

"Lake?" Shad repeated.

J.T.'s eyes grew large. "In the kitchen?"

Norma nodded. "It's forming Lake Superior." She looked around the bathroom, then left, shaking her head. "Sure is hard to get good help nowadays." They heard her chuckling to herself as she went down the hall.

J.T. crossed back into her bedroom, taking off her shoes. It didn't really help. "Don't worry. I can handle it," Shad assured her.

She had no doubts that he could. Hadn't she seen that he could handle anything that was thrown his way? Frankie, science projects. Her?

"If I didn't know any better, I'd say you were trying to find ways to keep working here," she teased.

"I wasn't the one who decided to use the interior of a toilet tank for show-and-tell," he reminded her.

She raised her chin regally. "I need to change."

He looked down at his sopping jeans. His shirt, hanging on the bathroom doorknob, had suffered the same fate. "That makes two of us. I've got a change of clothes in the car. Be back in a second."

You couldn't help but admire a man like that. "Always prepared, aren't you?"

He looked at her meaningfully, his eyes savoring the way her wet clothes brought out every single curve on her body. "No, not always." He was about to leave, then turned again. "One good thing, though."

"What?"

"The coffee stain is almost gone from your skirt."

She looked down and saw that he was right. "I guess there's a silver lining in every cloud."

"Those are the words I live by," he answered, leaving.

J.T. made her way to the closet, squishing as she went. Wouldn't it be wonderful, she thought, if she could really believe that? Somehow, she mused, selecting a fresh outfit, it seemed to be getting a little easier. At least as long as he was here.

Chapter Twelve

"So when is the dance?" J.T. asked Frankie.

She glanced up and saw Shad walking in through the back door to join them in the kitchen and smiled in response to his greeting. It seemed so natural to see him walk in like that.

He was now an integral part of her life. In such a short time he had managed to break through all her carefully constructed barriers. That was surely a danger sign. But he hadn't accomplished this as a seducer. He hadn't overwhelmed her with sexuality. He hadn't done anything but be there for her, for them. He hadn't taken advantage of her needs. But he had overwhelmed her with kindness, with the way he saw life.

Yet she was still uncertain. The pain last time had been so great, so deep. This time it might be different because *he* was different. But what if, for some reason, it didn't work out? What if it didn't work out even though he was so perfect? Then there would be no hope, absolutely no hope left. In her heart she knew she couldn't face that.

"This Saturday," Shad answered, picking up one of the bacon slices draining on the board beside Norma. Norma pushed the board closer to him and smiled her approval.

J.T. roused herself from her thoughts. "How do you keep track of everything?" His life was as full as hers, possibly more so. Yet everything that was important was underscored.

"Easy." He accepted the plate Norma pushed into his hand, heaped with scrambled eggs, toast and bacon. "You're an angel, Norma." The woman beamed as she busied herself with making Frankie's lunch. "I made a note of it when I penciled us in on the volunteer list."

J.T.'s juice threatened to back up. "Run this by me again?"

There was a knock on the back door, and Frankie reluctantly gathered up his books. Norma held out the lunch sack. Snaring it as he hurried out, Frankie said, "I gotta go. See you all later."

Shad straddled the chair next to J.T. as he sat down. There was no whiff of cologne, nothing but a very distinct scent that was his alone. J.T. felt something stir quickly and forced herself to keep her mind on the conversation, not on the closeness of his body.

"I saw the notice asking for volunteers on top of Frankie's textbook. So I volunteered us."

"Us?" she repeated dumbly. He couldn't have. Not even he would do that. She wasn't any good around a large gathering of teenagers. The very thought made her nervous.

"Yes." He went on eating as if he hadn't just tossed her into the lion's den. "I didn't think you'd want to go alone."

Why did he keep thinking he had the right to go crashing through her life like this, arranging things? "You take an awful lot upon yourself, McClellan."

He glanced up. "No more than I can handle."

She opened her mouth and then shut it again, at a loss. And then she realized that the fury she was gathering to her was dissipating instead. Why wasn't she angrier about this? He was purposely manipulating her life.

Because she wanted to go with him, that was why, she realized. Anticipation began to build. In an odd way it might even be fun.

Okay, so maybe this wasn't such a terrible thing he had done. But she wasn't about to let him off the hook so easily. "What if I'm busy?"

He raised his soulful eyes and looked into hers. He was good, very good, she thought. He had her totally disarmed in less than a heartbeat. "Too busy for your only son's first dance?"

"You're good at this guilt thing, aren't you?"

"The best. My foster mother is Italian. They have guilt down to an art form," he told her, thinking fondly of the woman who had loved him as her own. "Besides—" he took a sip of the coffee Norma poured for him, then cradled the cup between his hands "—I checked your calendar in your den. You're free."

"Anything you don't think of?"

He leaned so close that there wasn't enough room for a sigh. "Try me."

She closed her eyes to pull herself together. "Time to go to work."

"Just what I was thinking."

And she knew about what, too. Working on her undoing. What, oh, what was she going to do when this wonderfully infuriating man had moved on as she knew he would?

Careful, J.T., you're surrendering.

"Well, if I'm going to go to a 'dance,' I'd better get things settled at the office." She pushed back her chair from the table. "I'll be working late tonight, Norma," she announced.

Norma gave her a disapproving look, then quickly turned her back as Shad gathered J.T. close for a goodbye kiss.

J.T. walked out, lightning pulsating at all the important points of her body. She was going to miss that, too.

She didn't work late. Instead, she found herself delegating two accounts that she had always maintained as her exclusive property. Shad was right. The people who worked for her *were* competent. There was no reason in the world why she couldn't let go of some of the reins, ease up just a little. The business wouldn't fall apart if she wasn't maintaining constant vigil. The main crisis had passed, and she didn't have to keep guard, waiting for something else to go wrong. She had earned the right to kick back a little.

"Just in time!" Shad announced, taking her arm as she walked through the door.

As always, he made her head spin. He had that gift. And worse, she was getting to like this breathtaking ride on the merry-go-round. She dropped her briefcase onto the table. Frankie was at her elbow, shifting from foot to foot, eager to be off.

"Just in time for what?" J.T. asked.

"Frankie and I were going shopping for something for him to wear to the dance. Now that you're here we can all go."

She had planned on coaxing Frankie into this tomorrow morning. Shad was one step ahead of her. She might have known.

"We." She suddenly realized he had said "we" as if they were a unit. If only she could believe that. Maybe, just for a little while, as long as she remembered it was a temporary illusion, she could let herself go with it.

J.T. smiled.

He loved the way she smiled. "I take that as a resounding yes." Shad opened the door. "We'll be back in a couple of hours, Norma," he called to the kitchen.

He even thought of letting Norma know when to expect them. The man was one of a kind. "Certainly have taken over, haven't you?" J.T. asked.

"Just temporarily stepping in."

Temporarily. Just until Frankie seemed to be doing fine. And then he'd be gone. "Yes." Her smile faded to a shadow of what it had been as she walked out. "I know."

Three hours later they left the mall exhausted, armed with a suit that pleased Frankie, shoes and everything that went in between. Frankie's excitement was growing, and he forgot to be blasé about the upcoming dance.

"I keep saying thank you," J.T. said to Shad when they reached home.

Opening his trunk, he handed Frankie his clothing bag. Holding it aloft on the hanger, he hurried off to show Norma, while Shad helped J.T. with the other assorted bags and boxes.

"Not necessary," he told J.T. "I'm getting a big kick out of this." He slammed down the trunk. "Now, what are you going to wear?"

"Me?" She hadn't given it any thought. She had been too busy being nervous for Frankie. Someone had to be since Frankie seemed to be approaching this major first in his life with blissful abandonment.

Shad followed J.T. into the house. "Chaperones have to dress up, too, you know," he told her. Although if he had his choice, he would have liked to see her with very little on. Maybe just a single blue hair ribbon holding back her hair, tied loosely so that he could pull it free just before he made slow, exquisite love with her.

J.T. turned to see him looking at her. The warmth of his gaze ignited a kindred reaction within her. She felt as if she was going to the dance herself as a date, not a chaperone. She shrugged, trying to stay nonchalant. "I'll come up with something."

He put the bundles down on the sofa. "Want my help?"

"No," she said quickly, then realized that she wanted to keep it a surprise. Like a silly teenager, she mocked herself. Still, she couldn't help the bubble of excitement she felt building within her.

When she opened the door the following evening, it was to a Shad she hadn't met before. Seeing him in a navy blue suit with a pale blue shirt, opened at the throat, nearly took her breath away. Men in suits were supposed to look professional, competent; they weren't supposed to look teeth-clenching sexy. She just stood in the doorway, holding on to the doorknob and feeling flustered.

Norma whistled appreciatively from the hallway, bringing her out of her fog. "You're prettier than she is."

"Thank you." Shad laughed, walking in. J.T. backed up self-consciously. "You're gorgeous," he told J.T., and then enjoyed watching the color bloom in her face.

She bit her lower lip, tempting him to nibble on it, too. "Thank you." No doubt about it, she thought helplessly, she felt like a teenager, a shy, awkward teenager.

"These are for you," Shad told her.

"What is?"

He held up a white box. "The flowers."

Until then she hadn't realized he was holding anything. He had a box in one hand, a single white carnation in the other.

"For me?" Frankie looked at the flower dubiously. He was wearing what all the guys his age wore—baggy, pleated dark pants, an oversized dark shirt and a snow-white jacket, pushed up at the sleeves.

"Trust me, it's okay," Shad promised. Frankie shrugged, accepted the flower and poked it into position in his lapel. Then he flashed a grin at Shad. "Pretty cool, I'd say." Shad turned toward J.T. "Both of you."

J.T. flushed with pleasure. She was wearing her hair down. It fell full and luxuriant along her shoulders, the deep chestnut complementing the light blue of her dress. Her shoulders were bare. Shad ached to skim his fingers along her skin. And his lips.

"I wasn't sure what color you were wearing," he told J.T., handing her the box, "so I played it safe."

"Safe? You?"

He nodded. "It happens sometimes."

She opened the box to find three white roses fashioned into a corsage and nestled against green tissue paper. Tears welled up in her throat, making it difficult for her to catch her breath. "Oh, Shad."

He didn't want to make her cry. Did white roses remind her of something she wanted to forget? "Julienne, what's the matter?"

She shook her head, trying to turn away from him. "Nothing." The word was barely audible. She had never gotten a corsage before. Seeing it made her remember how much she had wanted to be asked to her senior prom. "I never went to my senior prom," she mumbled, feeling like a total idiot for letting him see how this affected her.

Shad raised her chin until she was forced to look into his eyes. "I know. Frankie told me. I thought maybe tonight we could pretend that this is your prom, too."

"Thank you," she whispered, kissing his cheek.

J.T. cleared her throat, aware that Frankie was solemnly watching this exchange. "C'mon, are we going to discuss ancient history, or get this show on the road?" She began to walk out, the box still in her hand.

"You can take it out of the box, Julienne," Shad prompted.

"I knew that." She started to remove the corsage from the box.

Shad placed his hand over hers. "Let me."

Then she held her breath as he pinned it to her dress. Her breast burned where he had lightly brushed it.

Frankie fiddled with his carnation. "C'mon. I promised to meet Karl at the dance. His dad's driving him."

Shad put his hand on Frankie's shoulder as they walked out and laughed. "By all means, let's hurry."

The gym was gaily decorated with balloons and streamers, its lighting subdued enough to make people forget the noise and cheers that usually echoed within its walls. The theme of the dance was simply "spring." It was enough. At one end a student band was playing surprisingly well. Songs that J.T. recognized from her own youth. She wondered if the band was playing them by their own choice or by the principal's. No matter. The effect was the same. She felt as if she had gone back in time.

Tapping her foot to a catchy tune, J.T. watched as Frankie approached a girl with long blond hair and the smile of an angel. The angel, J.T. realized, was smiling directly at her son. Frankie seemed to bloom right before her eyes. It wouldn't be long now. Her son was growing up. J.T. sighed.

"What's the matter?" Shad asked as he handed her a glass of bright red punch.

"Nothing. Just watching Frankie. He *is* having a good time, isn't he?"

He took a sip, tried not to make a face at the slightly thickened punch and set it down. "Looks like the hit of the dance to me."

"He has you to thank for that."

"I didn't make him handsome. Genes did that. Your genes."

J.T. looked down. His compliments had a way of making her fumble. Maybe because she had never had much practice at receiving them, she thought. "I meant that if you hadn't talked him into it at first, he wouldn't have had the courage to come out here."

"Oh, I think he would have eventually. He's got a lot of spunk." He pushed a curl from her shoulder, wishing they were alone. "Like his mom."

"Yeah," she said with a short, disparaging laugh. "His big, brave mom."

"No, not so big, but the rest is right. Julienne?"

"Hmm?" She was watching a boy gather up courage to ask the girl next to him for a dance. The suffering continued when the girl nodded. She was several inches taller, and neither one looked very comfortable. J.T. winced for them.

"Why didn't you go to your senior prom?"

She shrugged, still watching the mismatched pair. They were getting the hang of it. "I was too busy studying for finals to bother."

"No one ever asked?"

She shook her head. It seemed so far away. It shouldn't hurt anymore. But it did. "No, no one ever asked."

He took her cup from her hands and guided her away from the buffet table where they were standing. She looked at him, puzzled, but didn't protest. "I'm asking."

"Shad, I—"

"Will you say yes to a slightly old, trembling adolescent?"

"Trembling?" she repeated with a laugh.

"Every time I'm with you." His eyes were dark, serious. "Dance with me, Julienne?"

She looked around uncertainly. The floor was half-filled with teenagers, but as far as she could see, none of the adults were dancing. "I thought we were just supposed to observe."

He slipped one hand in hers as he encircled her waist with the other. Her dress whispered against him as her body leaned into his. "I distinctly remember the words 'mingling allowed' clearly being written on the form. I feel like mingling. With you."

"How can I say no?"

He grinned. "That's just the idea. You can't."

She leaned her cheek against his chest, letting him guide her, letting her senses go as a dreamy melody from the seventies surrounded them. It was so easy, so very easy to drift off, to pretend for a few minutes that this man was the right one, that he'd really stay in her life now that he was here.

Just for tonight she'd believe.

Dottie twisted in her chair at the sound of the front door opening. The gray-and-white Pomeranian jumped up, alert at her feet, poised to protect his mistress. "Prince Charming back so soon from the ball?"

Shad stooped to scratch Wolfgang behind the ear and was accosted by two other dogs of various heritages. Mutts just like he and Dottie, he thought fondly. "You didn't have to wait up."

"No, but I wanted to find out." Dottie's grin was impish. "How did the prom go?"

He sat down on the hassock, shrugging out of his jacket. "Are you playing mother?"

"I thought I'd practice." She tapped her cast. "Once this gets off I can take over with Frankie." She eyed him, waiting to be contradicted.

"You might not have to."

It was what she wanted to hear. "Oh?"

Mulligan Stew, the last dog Dottie had saved from the shelter, rested his long, pointy snout on Shad's lap expectantly. Shad obliged, stroking the silky head. When Dottie moved back to her apartment, Shad wasn't sure what he was going to do with his hands. "Julienne is finding ways to get closer and spend more time with Frankie."

"Out of a job before I even got a foot in the door, so to speak." She shifted, trying to get comfortable. "How about your foot?"

"Explanation?"

"Both planted firmly on the ground?"

He knew what she was driving at. For Dottie, this was unusually subtle. "I'm not sure." He rose. Mulligan yapped indignantly. "I know I care about her, about them."

"Care?"

"Yes, care. All right, a lot. Satisfied?"

"Yes."

He grew serious. "It's all happening so fast."

"Worried?"

"Maybe."

She studied him thoughtfully. "Why?"

"I want it happening for the right reasons. Frankly, I'm a little afraid I might be drawn to them because I want a family and they're here, ready-made." He lifted a shoulder, turning around. A third dog, Sweetie Pie, scurried away from underfoot. "That wouldn't be fair to Julienne. She's already been hurt once."

Dottie accepted Wolfgang's faithful allegiance, stroking the dog as she spoke. She wrinkled her brow, pondering Shad's words. "You're a do-gooder and a great guy, but I don't think your sense of charity goes that far. In case you haven't noticed, big brother, you've always had me. And, for most of our lives, we've had the Marinos, which, when you start counting the various foster uncles, aunts, cousins, not to mention big brother Angelo, I think we could say that our family is bordering on a crowd scene, wouldn't you?"

He shrugged as he picked up a doggy toy. Mulligan jumped up and caught it, ready for a tug-of-war. He was disappointed when Shad let him win so easily. "Maybe I'm just being nervous."

"Maybe. It's a big step that you're contemplating, isn't it?"

He cocked his head. "How do you know what I'm contemplating?"

"I've always been able to read you like a book. You're in love with her."

"Is it that evident?"

"It is to me. Heck, even Angelo can see it, and he has to be hit over the head with a two-by-four to notice things like that. C'mere." She held out her arms to him. "Don't make me get up to hug you, Shad. I just got comfortable in this chair."

He bent down, bracing his hands on the arms of the chair as she squeezed him tightly. "I'm very, very happy for you," Dottie told him.

"Don't count your rose blossoms before they fall, kid. The lady might have something to say about this."

Her eyebrows drew together beneath strawberry bangs that had a tendency to hang in her eyes. "Other than yes?"

"Other than yes."

"You didn't tell me she was stupid."

"Not stupid." He thought of the way Julienne's eyes filled with fear. It was something he promised himself he was going to find a way to erase. Permanently. "Just frightened."

"Hold on to her tightly when you propose. If you need a letter of recommendation, just let me know. And if she says no after that, I'll hit her upside her head and knock some sense into her."

He laughed out loud at the image that conjured up. "Always count on you to be subtle."

"Always." She settled back in the chair and clicked on the television set with the remote control. "Now go into the kitchen and make us some popcorn. They're showing our favorite movie on cable in ten minutes."

He tapped the long plaster cast with his fingers. "How long before this thing comes off?"

She looked up at him, smiling sweetly as she patted his cheek. The gesture was meant to be patronizing. "Not before the movie starts. Now feed me so that I have enough strength to dance at your wedding."

Shad went off to fill her request, followed by two of the dogs yapping at his heels. All of Dottie's dogs loved popcorn.

Chapter Thirteen

J.T. looked at the corsage in the refrigerator, a dreamy smile spreading over her lips as the memory of Friday night played itself out. If she closed her eyes, she could still feel Shad's arms around her, holding her as they danced in the gym.

"Hungry?"

Norma's voice startled her as the woman walked in. Hurriedly J.T. moved the corsage aside. "No. I just wanted some milk for my coffee." J.T. grabbed the container and shut the refrigerator door.

Norma eyed the empty coffee maker. The switch was on off. "Better make some coffee first," she advised. "I'm off to the cleaners."

J.T. merely nodded. The back door shut quietly behind the woman. All the squeaking, sticking doors had been dealt with. Shad had seen to that. Just as he had to everything else.

Feeling melancholy, J.T. returned the carton of milk to the refrigerator, telling herself she was foolish to mope like this. But she couldn't help it any more than she could help the empty, panicky feeling that was growing inside her.

With Frankie off with a friend and Norma on errands, J.T. was alone with Shad. Possibly for the last time, she thought. The work was done. Even she could see that. It was time to come to grips with things.

Jacobs had called her office this morning, telling her that his company had decided to hire her firm to handle their accounts. It meant a lot of extra business coming in. She should have felt elated. She didn't. Nothing seemed to matter except Shad.

She looked up when she heard him in the other room and quickly crossed over to the stairs. He was bringing the toolbox down, ready to store it in his car.

Say something, she thought in desperation. Make him stay.

"Finished?' Brilliant, J.T. The U.N. is going to be knocking down your door at any second, asking you to negotiate peace treaties around the world.

His shirt hanging loosely around his shoulders, unbuttoned, Shad set down the box. "Just need to clean up the powder room and that's that."

J.T. chewed on her bottom lip, thinking, grasping at straws. "You know, I've been thinking about getting a new roof put on."

Why didn't she realize that she didn't have to go through this charade? That she could be honest with him about her feelings? Were they still really strangers? Or was she so afraid of life that she was going to go on living lies? "How old is your present one?"

She lifted a shoulder. "As old as the house, I guess."

"Which is?"

"Eleven years." What did that have to do with it? Was he trying to find a way to turn her down? To tell her that he'd lost interest? That he had other things to do?

He wanted to hold her, to tell her that games were over. "I don't think you need a new one."

Translation, I'm leaving, she thought. No more excuses to hide behind, she thought. While he was working on the house he'd had to be there, and she'd had the best of both worlds: his presence without the necessity of her making a commitment. A commitment that would be the beginning of the end. Now he was finished and wouldn't be around every day. If she wanted things to continue between them, she was going to have to make a commitment. He wouldn't accept anything less. She knew that. The ramifications terrified her.

And what if it turned out to be out of sight, out of mind for him? What if, once he was working on something else, the novelty of being a "resident father figure" wore thin? What if he walked out on her the way Pete had?

No, not Shad.

And yet the fear wouldn't go, wouldn't leave her.

You grew to depend on someone emotionally, and you were always left high and dry.

In a fog she began to cross back to the kitchen. There was a corsage in the refrigerator that she needed to throw away.

Shad put his hand on her arm. He felt her stiffen. What was wrong? They couldn't possibly be back to square one. "I have something to discuss with you."

"Yes?" Here it came, she thought.

All right, now that he had her attention, how was he going to broach this when she looked so damn unapproachable again? You just didn't open up your heart to a woman who looked as if she would have been warm wearing a bikini in Nome.

The doorbell rang before he could find a way to get past the frost in her eyes. "Want to get that? I can finish later."

J.T. squared her shoulders and walked to the front door. What was she going to tell Frankie if he didn't come around anymore? Would relations between them deteriorate again? Frankie was still a teenager, still prone to "the terrible teens" that had brought about their schism to begin with. Nothing had really changed that much; nothing except having Shad in their lives.

And if he *wasn't* in their lives?

She was in no mood to talk to anyone, least of all the woman she found standing on the front step when she opened the door.

Adriana, every blond hair carefully in place, her designer sea-green suit perfectly molded to her body, stood in J.T.'s doorway, striking a pose for the world's benefit. Adriana, the reason no one ever remembered her name in school, J.T. thought. Her sister, older by two years, had always outshone her, being the stereotypical golden girl all through school.

J.T. mustered a smile. "Hi. What are you doing in my neck of the woods?"

Adriana waved an impatient hand toward her chauffeur, indicating that she wanted him to wait for her. Crossing into the room as if every movement was being monitored and memorized for future emulation, Adriana walked into the living room and looked around. The slight hint of disapproval was there as it always was.

"Well, I've been thinking about your problem." As she spoke, she looked Shad over carefully as if he were an inanimate object. Shad returned the compliment. Adriana haughtily averted her face, annoyed.

This was something new, J.T. thought. Adriana never concerned herself with J.T.'s life. The only words of con-

solation she had ever said when J.T. found herself alone
with Frankie was a smug "I told you so."

"What problem?" J.T. asked suspiciously.

"Why Francis, of course." Adriana glanced at the sofa
and apparently decided against sitting down. She wasn't
going to stay that long. "You sounded really disturbed
when I spoke to you two weeks ago."

J.T. remembered the call. It was Adriana who had called
her, asking her advice about some creative accounting that
her husband had been caught in. The conversation hadn't
ended well when J.T. said he'd have to suffer the consequences. "That was over a month ago," J.T. corrected.
"Why are you coming to talk to me now?"

"I was on my way to see my lawyer. Tyson has proven to
be very tiresome."

That would be divorce number three, J.T. thought. Obviously the creative accounting episode hadn't been re-
solved in Tyson's favor.

"Anyway—" Adriana opened her purse "—I thought
I'd show you these." She took out three brochures and
handed them to J.T.

J.T. looked at them, then back at her sister. Her expression was blank. "Why would I be interested in seeing
them?"

Adriana pursed her lips at her sister's stubbornness.
"They're the best boarding schools money can buy, dear."
Her tone was condescending. "Leslie and Alexis go to this
one." A jewel-encrusted hand tapped the top brochure.

Leslie and Alexis were her nieces. J.T. never got to see
them anymore. And neither, she knew, did her sister.

J.T. handed the brochures back to her sister. "I don't
want to send Frankie away."

"Frankie?" Adriana scowled. "Since when have you
started calling him that awful name?"

Shad could see why Julienne and her sister had never been close. The woman was certainly irritating the hell out of him. "Since he indicated that he preferred it." He moved next to J.T.

The small gesture warmed her. She had never had any support against her sister before. At home Adriana had always been the favored one, the one who did everything right.

"Who is this?" Cold, beautifully made-up eyes raked over him.

"Shad McClellan." J.T. didn't like Adriana's attitude when she looked at him. It was the same way she looked at everyone who wasn't old money. "He's here renovating my bathrooms."

"Oh." The single word dripped with disdain. J.T. curbed a desire to physically throw her sister out.

With a regal movement of her shoulders Adriana blocked Shad out completely. "I think you should consider these. Francis is wild, he's hyper, he's—"

"Normal?" Shad suggested.

There was affronted indignation in Adriana's eyes. "Julienne, are you in the habit of letting the help interrupt your private conversations?"

"Only when they make sense," J.T. snapped. Breeding only went so far.

Adriana's small, perfect mouth dropped open as she stared at her sister. J.T. had never talked back to her. "I think I've just been insulted."

Years of suffering snide remarks and belittling words came to a boiling point.

"Adriana, if you don't know an insult when it stares you in the face, you're even more narcissistic than I thought you were." J.T. began moving forward, like a panther stalking its prey. Shaken, Adriana took a step back and then another, but J.T. kept coming. Shad watched, amused and silently cheering her on. "I don't need your advice, your snobbish opinions, or your presence in my house any longer until you learn to behave like a human being instead of a goddess slumming among the peasants." They were at the front door. "Now, until you change your attitude, until you show Shad some proper respect, you're not welcome in my house and I'll thank you to get out of it!"

Adriana glared at Shad, utterly stunned. "What the hell does he have to do with it?"

"Everything," J.T. shouted back, her words coming faster than her ability to think through the consequences. "He's made my life worth living for the first time in years, and I love him!"

"Him?" Adriana's scathing look had absolutely no effect on Shad. "Then you're an even bigger idiot than I thought you were! I'll see myself out!" Adriana stumbled over the threshold as she took another step away from J.T. The younger woman's expression was almost menacing.

"No, let me!" J.T. slammed the door in her sister's face.

She felt Shad's hands on her shoulders. "Julienne, did you mean that?"

"Yes! She's always been a royal, pompous pain, and I've wanted to tell her off for years. It feels glorious."

He turned her around slowly. "That's not the part I was talking about."

Her face flushed from the confrontation, she looked up at him, suddenly realizing her mistake. She had admitted loving him. He probably thought her a fool. "I said a lot of things in the heat of the moment."

"Was that all it was? Just the heat of the moment?" His eyes wouldn't let her lie to either of them.

"No, all right? Are you satisfied?" She tried to shrug out of his grasp.

"No, but I will be." His mouth crushing hers, he kissed her long and hard, draining the struggle from her. That slight barrier he had always been aware of was gone. The wall was down.

She felt as if she were standing before a fireplace and letting the flames in the hearth warm her inch by inch. The kiss melted her until she was sure her entire body could have been poured into an eight-ounce water glass.

No, she told herself, she couldn't just go with these feelings anymore. She had to think. She wasn't going to let this go on, for whatever reason, only to let it end abruptly in a week or two, or nine.

He felt the hesitation return. "Julienne—"

She broke away, shaking her head. "No, let me talk."

He crossed his arms, resigned. "All right. Say what you need to say." If it's no, it's not going to do you any good, he promised silently.

When she did speak, her voice was subdued, calm, but he heard the pain that the words were trying to hide. "I was very hungry for love when I was a girl. My parents never showed any. It wasn't their way. And you just met Adriana." A sad smile played on her lips. He wanted to hold her, but knew he couldn't yet. She had to get this out. "I married the first person who said he loved me. I realize now that he loved me in his own fashion, the way he loved his car, the way he loved getting out and driving, the way he loved a good glass of wine." She dragged a hand through her hair, then let it fall. "I tried to make it work because I thought the problem had to do with me, not with him."

Overcome, she turned away and looked out the window. Taking a deep breath, J.T. pushed on. "And then one day he just looked at me and said, 'Hey, babe, I can't.' That was all. Just 'I can't.' And then he was gone. It was up to me to figure out that he meant can't be confined, can't be a husband, can't be a father. He never elaborated. The pain almost killed me. I really don't think I could handle it again.''

He had waited out her explanation. There was nothing there to make him change his mind. Gently Shad took her into his arms and turned her around. "Hey, babe," he whispered softly, "I can."

J.T. felt the tears rising. "But for how long?"

"Forever."

She looked back at the toolbox. "But you were leaving."

"Leaving?" He saw what she was looking at. "I'm just cleaning up. Leaving?" he repeated in wonder. "Lady, you'd have to sandblast me out of your life."

She laughed, relieved. "I was never very good with my hands."

He thought of the way her hands had felt against his skin, how the lightest touch had made his gut tighten. "I think you're very good with your hands." He kissed her temple, loving the scent tangled in her hair. "I'd get down on my knees and do it right, Julienne, but I've been on my knees all day, finishing the floor. Would you settle for an informal proposal?"

"No." Her smile was deep and wide and heartfelt. There were happy endings. And he was hers. "I don't think so." She entwined her arms around his neck. "I don't think I'd be settling at all. And the answer is yes. In nine-foot letters."

As he lowered his lips to hers again, they heard the back door slam. Norma walked into the room, several bundles in her arms. Frankie followed in her wake, then stopped dead. And grinned. Norma nodded her approval. "I take it you're planning on staying for dinner?" she asked Shad.

Shad looked down at the woman in his arms, the woman he had been searching for all his life. "Yes," he answered Norma. "From now on."

He vaguely thought he heard Frankie cheer, "All right," but he wasn't certain. He was too preoccupied at the moment to check it out.

* * * * *

Silhouette 🌹 *Romance*®

COMING NEXT MONTH

#820 PILLOW TALK—Patricia Ellis
Written in the Stars
Kendall Arden had made a big mistake in getting involved with
Jared Dalton's research on sleep. How could she confess her sensual
dreams to this oh-so-dedicated Libra man? Especially since he was the
subject of her fantasies....

#821 AND DADDY MAKES THREE—Anne Peters
Eric Schwenker firmly believed that a mother's place was at home, so why
was Isabel Mott using *his* office to care for her daughter? Maybe Isabel
could teach him about working mothers...and what a family truly was.

#822 CASEY'S FLYBOY—Vivian Leiber
Cautious Casey Stevens knew what she wanted—a decent, *civilized* home
for her baby. But sexy flyboy Leon Brodie tempted her to spread her wings
and fly. The handsome pilot was a good reason to let herself soar....

#823 PAPER MARRIAGE—Judith Bowen
Justine O'Malley was shocked by rancher Clayton Truscott's marriage
proposal—but then, so was he. Clayton had sworn never to trust a woman
again. But to keep his brother's children, he would do anything—
even *marry*!

#824 BELOVED STRANGER—Peggy Webb
Belinda Stubaker was incensed! Her employer, Reeve Lawrence, was
acting like Henry Higgins—insisting on teaching her the finer things in
life. How could Belinda explain to Reeve that *love* was the finest thing
there was....

#825 HOME FOR THANKSGIVING—Suzanne Carey
One kiss, so many years ago. Now, Dr. Aaron Dash and Kendra Jenkins
were colleagues at the same hospital. But that kiss could never be
forgotten. Beneath their professionalism, an intense passion
still lingered....

AVAILABLE THIS MONTH:

#814 THROUGH MY EYES
Helen R. Myers

#815 MAN TROUBLE
Marie Ferrarella

#816 DANCE UNTIL DAWN
Brenda Trent

#817 HOMETOWN HERO
Kristina Logan

#818 PATCHWORK FAMILY
Carla Cassidy

#819 EVAN
Diana Palmer

Silhouette Romance®

LONG, TALL TEXANS

EVAN
Diana Palmer

Diana Palmer's bestselling LONG, TALL TEXANS series continues with EVAN....

Anna Cochran is nineteen, blond and beautiful—and she wants Evan Tremayne. Her avid pursuit of the stubborn, powerfully built rancher had been a source of amusement in Jacobsville, Texas, for years. But no more. Because Evan Tremayne is about to turn the tables...and pursue her!

Don't miss EVAN by Diana Palmer, the eighth book in her LONG, TALL TEXANS series. Coming in September...only from Silhouette Romance.

SRLTT

SILHOUETTE®
OFFICIAL SWEEPSTAKES
RULES

NO PURCHASE NECESSARY

1. To enter, complete an Official Entry Form or 3" × 5" index card by hand-printing, in plain block letters, your complete name, address, phone number and age, and mailing it to: Silhouette Fashion A Whole New You Sweepstakes, P.O. Box 9056, Buffalo, NY 14269-9056.

   No responsibility is assumed for lost, late or misdirected mail. Entries must be sent separately with first class postage affixed, and be received no later than December 31, 1991 for eligibility.

2. Winners will be selected by D.L. Blair, Inc., an independent judging organization whose decisions are final, in random drawings to be held on January 30, 1992 in Blair, NE at 10:00 a.m. from among all eligible entries received.

3. The prizes to be awarded and their approximate retail values are as follows: Grand Prize — A brand-new Ford Explorer 4×4 plus a trip for two (2) to Hawaii, including round-trip air transportation, six (6) nights hotel accommodation, a $1,400 meal/spending money stipend and $2,000 cash toward a new fashion wardrobe (approximate value: $28,000) or $15,000 cash; two (2) Second Prizes — A trip to Hawaii, including round-trip air transportation, six (6) nights hotel accommodation, a $1,400 meal/spending money stipend and $2,000 cash toward a new fashion wardrobe (approximate value: $11,000) or $5,000 cash; three (3) Third Prizes — $2,000 cash toward a new fashion wardrobe. All prizes are valued in U.S. currency. Travel award air transportation is from the commercial airport nearest winner's home. Travel is subject to space and accommodation availability, and must be completed by June 30, 1993. Sweepstakes offer is open to residents of the U.S. and Canada who are 21 years of age or older as of December 31, 1991, except residents of Puerto Rico, employees and immediate family members of Torstar Corp., its affiliates, subsidiaries, and all agencies, entities and persons connected with the use, marketing, or conduct of this sweepstakes. All federal, state, provincial, municipal and local laws apply. Offer void wherever prohibited by law. Taxes and/or duties, applicable registration and licensing fees, are the sole responsibility of the winners. Any litigation within the province of Quebec respecting the conduct and awarding of a prize may be submitted to the Régie des loteries et courses du Québec. All prizes will be awarded; winners will be notified by mail. No substitution of prizes is permitted.

4. Potential winners must sign and return any required Affidavit of Eligibility/Release of Liability within 30 days of notification. In the event of noncompliance within this time period, the prize may be awarded to an alternate winner. Any prize or prize notification returned as undeliverable may result in the awarding of that prize to an alternate winner. By acceptance of their prize, winners consent to use of their names, photographs or their likenesses for purposes of advertising, trade and promotion on behalf of Torstar Corp. without further compensation. Canadian winners must correctly answer a time-limited arithmetical question in order to be awarded a prize.

5. For a list of winners (available after 3/31/92), send a separate stamped, self-addressed envelope to: Silhouette Fashion A Whole New You Sweepstakes, P.O. Box 4665, Blair, NE 68009.

PREMIUM OFFER TERMS

To receive your gift, complete the Offer Certificate according to directions. Be certain to enclose the required number of "Fashion A Whole New You" proofs of product purchase (which are found on the last page of every specially marked "Fashion A Whole New You" Silhouette or Harlequin romance novel). Requests must be received no later than December 31, 1991. Limit: four (4) gifts per name, family, group, organization or address. Items depicted are for illustrative purposes only and may not be exactly as shown. Please allow 6 to 8 weeks for receipt of order. Offer good while quantities of gifts last. In the event an ordered gift is no longer available, you will receive a free, previously unpublished Silhouette or Harlequin book for every proof of purchase you have submitted with your request, plus a refund of the postage and handling charge you have included. Offer good in the U.S. and Canada only.

SLFW · SWPR

SILHOUETTE® OFFICIAL SWEEPSTAKES ENTRY FORM

4-FWSRS-2

Complete and return this Entry Form immediately – the more entries you submit, the better your chances of winning!

- Entries must be received by **December 31, 1991.**
- A Random draw will take place on **January 30, 1992.**
- No purchase necessary.

Yes, I want to win a FASHION A WHOLE NEW YOU Sensuous and Adventurous prize from Silhouette:

Name _____ Telephone _____ Age _____

Address _____

City _____ State _____ Zip _____

Return Entries to: **Silhouette FASHION A WHOLE NEW YOU,**
P.O. Box 9056, Buffalo, NY 14269-9056 © 1991 Harlequin Enterprises Limited

PREMIUM OFFER

To receive your free gift, send us the required number of proofs-of-purchase from any specially marked FASHION A WHOLE NEW YOU Silhouette or Harlequin Book with the Offer Certificate properly completed, plus a check or money order (do not send cash) to cover postage and handling payable to Silhouette FASHION A WHOLE NEW YOU Offer. We will send you the specified gift.

OFFER CERTIFICATE

Item	A. SENSUAL DESIGNER VANITY BOX COLLECTION (set of 4) (Suggested Retail Price $60.00)	B. ADVENTUROUS TRAVEL COSMETIC CASE SET (set of 3) (Suggested Retail Price $25.00)
# of proofs-of-purchase	18	12
Postage and Handling	$3.50	$2.95
Check one	☐	☐

Name _____

Address _____

City _____ State _____ Zip _____

Mail this certificate, designated number of proofs-of-purchase and check or money order for postage and handling to: **Silhouette FASHION A WHOLE NEW YOU Gift Offer,** P.O. Box 9057, Buffalo, NY 14269-9057. Requests must be received by December 31, 1991.

ONE PROOF-OF-PURCHASE

4-FWSRP-2

To collect your fabulous free gift you must include the necessary number of proofs-of-purchase with a properly completed Offer Certificate.

© 1991 Harlequin Enterprises Limited

See previous page for details.